It' The Hood in Him:

A Real N*gga Stole My Heart

Written By:

Jamie Marie

To submit a manuscript for our review email us at

kellzkpublishing@gmail.com

Join our mailing list to get a notification when Kellz K Publishing has another release!

Text KKP to 22828 to join

Dedication

This book is dedicated to my mother Paulette Jackson. You always encouraged me to go after what I wanted and never settle for less. I pray that I have made you proud by not giving up and following thru on my dreams. My kids my biggest inspiration. Through long days and sleepless nights you two pushed me, by always telling me that I am the best mom ever. My best friend in the whole world I love you beyond the moon. The ladies of KKP you all will forever hold a special place in my heart. Kellz, Chan, Mya, Niyah, Eboni, Nayh and Shameeka. Thank you all for encouraging me. My big brothers I love you two forever. Lastly my city (Sumter, SC) Thank you all for the love.

Love is an emotion that everyone feels at some point in their life. Love can bring you joy and pain. Finding love is hard, but it's not impossible. You have to know what you looking for in a lover. It's an energy you feel when love strikes. Love may come from someone you least expect it to come from. You may think you know, but love is tricky.

DARIUS THOMAS

"**D**J where you at, nigga?" I heard Zay call out.

"I'm in the kitchen, nigga. Why you yellin' my name like that?"

"I've been calling ya ass for the last twenty minutes. You gotta get them ears cleaned, playboy. No bitch likes a nigga with wax clogged ears."

"Tell that to the bitch I bagged last night. I was on the phone with her setting shit up for tonight."

"Fuck bitches, nigga! We're about to do this job and come up on some real money. Pussy can wait."

"Nah, my pops can wait. Money ain't going nowhere cause we them niggas making moves in the city. Don't shit shake unless we sign off on it."

"All facts but a nigga still not tryna be late," he said then walked away.

I was serious bout letting my father wait because he was caught up on micromanage shit. My father Leon 'Big L' Thomas ran shit in the DMV area. He was the king, and I was the prince of this street shit. I was ready to move his old ass off the throne and take my rightful seat, but he wasn't with the shits. At twenty, he didn't feel I was ready. In his mind, there was no need for a twenty-year-old to be seeing the type of money I was trying to see. I was the perfect age to take shit over, and I was young enough not to be set in my ways and absorb everything he taught me. I was old enough to fuck a nigga up behind my money and make the hard calls. I was the fruit of his labor, so how in the fuck was I not ready. I had it all on lock— money, respect, and plenty of pussy. The only thing I was lacking was the power. Power only came when you had the title to match, and I was working on that shit.

Running out the door after sending a text, I called out to Zay, "Nigga, you out here yelling for me, but where the hell are you?"

"I'm right here waiting on your slow ass. Stop tryna mack to the baddies and bring ya ass on."

"Man, shit, ya begging for the pussy ass up. I lay my game down, and these hoes fall to their knees."

"How you gonna say I be begging for pussy when ya ass beg more than these whining ass R&B singers out here?" We both laughed and got into my car.

Despite all the shit I was talking, I had never been a flashy nigga. When I was around my boys, yeah I boasted bout the shit I had cause I knew them niggas were solid. I learned early on that all that flashy shit could attract the wrong attention and leave you slumped somewhere. My black on black Charger was all I need. I kept it simple rocking the custom diamond chain that my father got me for my sixteenth birthday. It had my initials on it, and I was cool with that shit. I still got bitches with that shit, but my pimp game was strong cause I had the gift of gab. I could talk a hoe out of her panties and have her pussy leaking with no more than twenty words. I was blessed and had no one but my parents and the man above to thank for that.

"So, what's with shorty is she gone let your begging ass slide through? I know the hoe said yes."

"Of course she said yes, my nigga. Who am I?"

"You a cocky motherfucker is what you are." Zay laughed.

"Not cocky, I just know the type of nigga I am, and these bitches can't deny that."

"That's what you call cocky, my nigga."

"Nah, I call that shit confidence. Get like me and hoes may give you some play too."

"I get hoes. I just refuse to beg for them like you do, Darius."

"Gone with that Darius shit, Xavier." I laughed.

"Fuck you, nigga."

We pulled up to Big L's loft in about twenty minutes, and my mind went straight into business mode. We were meeting a new connect and wanted to make sure everything was legit before business was handled. My pops always taught me that when handling business you must always remain focused on your surroundings. Zay and I looked at each other before powering off our phones and placing them in the cup holder. We stepped out the car, made sure we were pistol ready, and then walked into the loft.

"There you are, son," Big L's deep raspy voice acknowledged when we walked in.

"What's good, pops?"

"You know what it is son business as usual."

"What's up, Big L?"

"Xavier, you ready to work?"

I'm always ready to make this paper."

"That's what I love to hear."

"So pops, who is this new connect we're meeting with?"

"In due time son, but first, how are things on the streets?"

"You know how it is, pops. Business is business and money is booming in. You know what shit is hitting for."

"You know I know young buck, but don't get too cocky in these streets. It only takes a second for a bullet to take you out and for your spot to get taken."

"Pops, I'm not worried about none of that shit. I'm always ten steps ahead. Before a nigga can think about getting at me, his ass is already got."

After a few more minutes of talking to Big L, I noticed a black and silver Bugatti pulling up.

"Who the fuck is that?"

"Damn, that bitch clean!" Zay said.

"That would be our new connect, Emmanuel."

"Pops, you know I am not with all that flashy shit."

"Trust me. This will make all of us a lot of money."

"Big L, my man, how is it going?" Emmanuel said, walking up on us.

"What's good, my friend?" my pops greeted.

"Just trying to make some money. Hopefully, your team can assist with that." He smirked. "You must be the infamous DJ, Prince of the DMV."

I sucked my teeth cause I already knew what this nigga was trying to do. I didn't need no hype because I was the fucking hype."

"Cut out all that infamous bullshit and let's just get down to business."

"Just what I like to see, a young man about his money. Ok young blood, let's talk figures."

***

An hour later Zay and I were back in my car headed back uptown.

"So what are you thinking, man? You've been quiet since we left your pops place."

"I don't know, Zay. Something's off bout that nigga. He came correct with them numbers, but his energy funny."

"The deal seems legit, DJ. It can make us a lot of money, and we can finally invest in this club business."

"I guess you right, man. Let's make this paper, my nigga."

"You already know money is my main bitch, DJ."

"Let's ride through and see how business is booming before we get ready to make this move tonight," I told him then plugged my phone up to the aux.

"Man, why in the hell you always riding to that sappy ass love music? You're a street nigga. You're not R Kelly, my nigga."

"Nigga, this is Boyz II Men, not R. Kelly stupid. Riding round to trap music ain't gon' do shit but have you out here treatin' bitches like hoes. That's why ya game is trash. You gotta listen to the oldies to learn how to talk to a female."

"These hoe's don't want to hear that shit, man. All these hoes care about is money, bundles, and dick. Breezy said it best... these hoes ain't loyal."

"Stop looking at these hoes and wife you a woman. I might be out here fucking hoes, but I know what I want my wife to be like."

"Oh yeah, what's that, nigga?"

"I want a woman that wants something out of life, and someone that I can build an empire and raise a family with. I can't do none of that shit fucking hoes."

"I get all that, but for now, a nigga is young and out here wildin'."

I nodded my head at his response cause there was no point in going back and forth. He felt how he felt, and it took a different type of maturity to understand where the fuck I was coming from.

IMANI PETERS

"**L**et's hit up this party tonight, Imani. I heard there will be hella niggas in the in there tonight.

"I don't know, Bri. I have to study for my medical terminology class."

"Imani, I hardly get see you as it is. Please come with me."

"Fine, you crybaby. We can meet at my place since it's closer to the house and you can get dressed here."

"That is perfect. Will your fine ass brother be there?"

"Brianna, don't start that shit. You know my brother is a hoe and will only play you and leave you."

"Whatever Imani, one day I will not only be your best friend, I will be your sister-in-law. Watch me, sis."

My best friend Brianna was always trying to get me to go out to random parties with her, knowing that house parties, or parties for that matter, are not my thing. I have always been the homebody, shy, always studying type. Now don't get me wrong. I will step out on occasions so that when I did step, I stepped the right way. Brianna was one of my personal stylists and would always make sure that I looked damn good.

"Look, Bri. I will go to this party with you, but I am not trying to stay all night, and I need you to help me find something to wear."

Jamie Marie

"Imani, you already know I'm gone get you right. I'm trying to get you fucked tonight."

"Don't start that shit. My body is a temple, and the right man will come along soon enough, and be allowed to open this treasure."

Yes, it's true I am still a virgin. Despite what people say, it's not a bad as you think. I just don't believe in letting anybody come up in me. Don't get it twisted. I have had this kitty played with and even toyed with oral sex, but a man has never sexed me, and honestly speaking, I am in no rush. I have an older brother, I have seen him with different girls every day, and I will not be one of those females who will settle for any man's dick.

"Well, if you're not trying to get fucked, I for damn sure am. Girl, I am dick deprived at the moment. The last dick I had was Aaron, and his shit was weak as fuck. I need me a monster dick that's gone put me to sleep for two days."

"Whatever Bri meet me at my place at nine. I'll be here."

I hung up the phone with Brianna and decided to do a little studying. School was very important to me, and I just had to be the best. It sounds completely whack, but growing up with parents like mine, you learn early the importance of education.

***

Later that night Brianna arrived at my house with everything that she needed to get us right for the night. Brianna chose for me a black, sheer romper that was sexy as hell, and my black Louis red bottoms were killing the shoe game right now. I don't like a lot of jewelry so my custom made "I" chain is always a must have along with my princess cut diamond studs. The one thing I didn't let Bri touch was my hair. I was ten years in this natural hair game, and I finally had my hair pattern the way I wanted it. So for tonight, a simple twist out would have to do. A little nude Mac lip gloss, and I was ready.

"Imani, you look beautiful."

"Thank you, Bri, You look hot, girl."

Now Brianna had a body that most bitches would love to pay for. She was stacked in all the right places, and anything she wore clung to her body like a glove, not a winter wool glove but like a latex glove. Tonight she was in a black, strapless mini dress with a pair of Gucci pumps. My best friend was fine, and she knew it.

"Girl, I know. Now let's go get our party on."

***

The drive to the party that Brianna just had to go to you could hear the music a mile away. The party was out in Rockville Maryland, about thirty minutes away from my apartment. House parties were definitely not my favorite, but for my best friend, I'd do just about anything.

"Imani, this party is about to be lit as fuck girl."

"Bri, you think every party is lit."

"That's because best friend I am a lit bitch and everywhere go is lit."

I couldn't help but laugh at Bri. She was dead ass serious.

"Damn, they shut about five streets down for this shit."

We arrived at the party in my midnight blue 2017 Impala. Stepping out, we both made sure we had our phones. We never leave without our phone. Brianna and I always made a promise that if either of us left without the other to always make sure to call once we reached our destination and always call the next morning. You could never be too safe.

I had to admit this party was packed from wall to wall. Liquor bottles were lined out on multiple tables along with various snacks and food. The music was definitely jumping. I mingled a little with a few folks that I knew from school, nothing major, but then I just happened to lay my eyes on the sexiest creature I'd ever seen. This man was fine. His eyes seemed like they were staring right into my soul. Yeah, I know what I said earlier, but this man would surely make me rethink my views on men. Those light brown eyes, deep dimples, and the waves would make anybody seasick.

"Imani, they're playing our shit. Let's go, bitch."

"Oh my god Bri, you are so extra."

"Extra? Bitch, bring your ass."

I followed Bri to the dance floor as "Sex With Me" by Rihanna played loudly through the speakers. It was like my eyes wouldn't leave this man. The more I danced, the more I fanaticized of him on the floor with me. Rihanna was speaking to me because I really wanted sex with him. The way he watched me all while smoking his blunt and biting his bottom lip had a bitch getting moist.

"Instead of eye fucking him, go over there and say something to him, Mani."

"Bri, I am not going over there to look like a fool. He's probably got females all over this party."

"Girl, they way y'all eye-fucking each other, if he does have a bitch here, she is nowhere near on that nigga's mind. That nigga wants you, and I suggest you step before a bitch like me steps to his fine ass, and I bet he's packing."

"Brianna, I am not going over there."

"And why the fuck not, Imani?"

"Because I'm not, I'm good honestly."

"Well, fuck it. If you don't, I will cause a bitch is horny. His friend is fine, god damn."

I just couldn't bring myself to approach him. A nigga like him had plenty of females and had access to plenty of pussy, so I would just be another one on his radar and end up getting hurt. Nah, I'm good with just looking. I turned back around, and my intuitions were right. He was here with someone. I watched as a beautiful female walked up to him and whispered something in his ear, and whatever it was had his full attention. He was fine, but I wasn't his type, I could only dream of a man like him, plus I wouldn't fit his lifestyle. I don't know why I set myself up to come to these parties. I was ready to go back to my place in my comfort zone.

DARIUS

amn, shorty was the shit, Zay."

"Yeah, shorty was bad. You need to find out who she is."

"Hell yeah," was all I could say.

Shorty was the shit. She had beautiful eyes, and everything on that body looked real. She didn't have the biggest ass, but what little she did have was placed perfectly. I could definitely see her on my arm running shit. She didn't seem like the females I fucked with on a regular, but I could see myself with her.

"The bitch she was with was fine too, my nigga."

"Fuck yeah she was fine, but she didn't have nothing on shorty tho."

The party was jumping, and there were bitches everywhere, but I was desperately in need of another blunt, I had to have my daily dose of the good shit.

"Let's go roll this blunt, nigga."

"Aight DJ, but don't roll that lil skinny shit. You be rolling shit that look like a damn toothpick. Who the fuck can get high off that shit?"

"Man, fuck you Xavier and come the fuck on before you don't get none of my shit."

"Shit Darius, you acting like that's gone faze me. You know I keep some loud in the stash."

Zay and I sat in my car passing the blunt back and forth and just enjoying that shit. The night was beautiful, and all that was missing was a bad bitch in my bed naked waiting on me to come and break her fucking back in. Pussy to me came a dime a dozen. Bitches were always throwing pussy at a nigga like me.

Like Janae, shorty I met at the club the other night, the bitch was bad with a big ass, huge fucking titties and was throwing the pussy the first night. I wasn't hurting in the pussy department, but a female like shorty from the party, she didn't look like the type to fuck on the first night. You had to work for that, and I wouldn't mind working for it. The plan tonight was to set up this lil meeting with my boys then meet with Janae and probably take her out to get some food, take her to a hotel, and fuck her world up. A bitch like Janae was all about what a nigga can do for her.

"Yo nigga, you talk to Kase about this move we trying to make?"

Kase was our other homie running this street shit with us. That nigga Kase was a smart nigga. He was currently going to Howard for business, which would come in handy once we were ready to turn this money legal.

"Nah I haven't talked to that nigga today. Knowing him, he's somewhere up Kaya's ass begging her not to leave."

"Nigga you crazy, Zay. How you gone tell that man business like that?"

"Shit, it's true. I ain't ever seen a nigga cheat so much on his bitch, but be bout to have a fucking heart attack when she leaves his ass. Shit, a nigga like me gets plenty of women, but the difference between Kase's crybaby ass and me is I am not committed to anyone. This nigga got a whole bitch who he asked to be his bitch, by the way, and still cheats. To be a smart nigga, that nigga is dumb."

"Man, text that nigga and tell him to meet us a Destiny. We got business to discuss."

"He said he would be there in ten minutes."

"Aight lets ride."

Zay and I cruised our city with the windows down bumping that new Mario. Unlike the majority of these street niggas, I was an R&B connoisseur. I didn't listen to trap music like most niggas did. Yeah, of course, you would bob to it in the club, but I didn't ride to it. I would have to thank my pops for that because he always had good R&B music playing whenever I would ride with him, and that shit really grew on a nigga. Don't let the R&B fool you tho. I was still a hard as nigga, and I didn't mind letting my trigga finger speak if need be.

My fucking city was beautiful. DC was my turf, but I wanted more. I had a plan, and my plan consisted of running the entire east coast in about a year. My pops didn't know this, but I was already making a name for myself in the Carolinas. I would often send Kase down there to make runs, being that his family is from Charlotte and shit.

"Damn, that nigga beat us here."

"I figured he would. Kaya's house is right down the street." I laughed.

"Zay, don't get that nigga started on Kaya."

"Trust me I won't. The last thing I want to hear is him bitching about her."

"Kase, what's up my nigga? Where the fuck you been hiding out at all day?"

"Shit, down at the school and at my folk's house."

"That's what's up but let's go in to discuss some shit."

"Aight, but whose car is that right there?"

"That might be that nigga Marcus' car, and if so then that works out perfectly. I can talk to both of y'all at the same time."

We all walked into Destiny to hold our lil meeting. Destiny was our main trap houses. That's where we kept eighty percent of our merchandise and money. On the outside, you would never know that Destiny was a trap house because it was located in one of the nicer areas in DC. Remember when I said earlier that I wasn't the flashy type. Well, that works to my advantage when I come through. I don't draw attention to myself, and all my niggas who came through Destiny was on the same page I was.

"Mark, my nigga, what's good?"

"Ain't shit, DJ. I'm just counting this product before I head to the house."

"My dude is always working. That's the shit I like."

"You know it. If I wanna eat I gotta put in the work."

"Hell yeah, so now that we are all here, we got a little bit of business to discuss."

I ran down the plan with Kase and Mark, and they were all on board. This takeover was going to make my team and me a lot of money, and of course, give me the power that I deserve. I was a street nigga at heart, and I worked hard at putting a solid team together and building a foundation. I trusted these niggas with my life, especially Zay. We all agreed that it was time to take over the DMV and beyond.

"So DJ, you really go take over from Big L?"

"What you mean? Hell yeah, I am taking over from my pops. I mean he's been running this shit for years, and it's time for him to step down and let the prince take over.

"Yeah, Big L taught us everything we know about this drug game, but what if he is not ready to step down?"

"Kase, you let me handle my pops. We doing this shit, and there is no turning back."

"The night is still young, so what y'all trying to do?" Kase asked.

"I'm about to go holla at Janae for a lil minute then take it back to the crib.

"What about you, Zay?"

"Shit, bout to hit this strip club and find me a stripper to take home and fuck."

"Shit, let's do it then."

"Man, you better take your ass back to Kaya for she has your ass crying again."

"Man fuck you, Zay. Kaya will be all right. Let's go."

I dapped up my boys and headed back to the party to scoop Janae. I sent her a text to make sure she was outside. I wasn't trying to go back in there. Pulling back up to the house the party was being held, that shit was still jumping. I didn't see Janae at first, but I did see shorty from earlier, and it looked like she was leaving. *Damn, she should have been leaving with me.* She was so fucking beautiful. We locked eyes, and her eyes were fucking mesmerizing. Maybe it was the weed, but I swear her eyes were calling me over there.

"Damn DJ, if you stare any harder, you gone stare a hole in the bitch."

"Shut the fuck up and get in, Janae."

"You staring her down like you trying to fuck her and shit."

"You can stay ya ass here if you gone be bitching the whole fucking time."

"What the fuck ever, DJ."

The one thing I can't stand is a nagging ass female. I swear Janae was about to piss me off, and I was gone fuck round and take her ass home, but I need my dick sucked, so fuck it.

Janae and I ended up at a local seafood restaurant out in Rockville. The conversation wasn't much other than the usual conversation from females. I mostly tuned her out. My mind was on shorty tho. She should have been the one here with me. Janae was fine no doubt, but I was ready to find my queen to settle with and give me a son to carry on the legacy I was building.

"You ready to go?" I asked Janae.

"Where are we going, your place?"

"Fuck it, yeah." I don't usually take females to my place, but fuck it. I wasn't in the mood to fuck with no motel and wanted to be in my own bed. I just hope she didn't take this shit seriously.

KASEEM PETERS

Walking into my parents' house, like always, my moms had the place smelling amazing. It was the twins' sixteenth birthday, and like every other birthday, my mother was cooking their favorite dishes. My mother was the original OG in the kitchen. When I tell you she put her foot in any meal she cooked, she played no games. Growing up everyone thought my mother was a professional chef, but nope, she was far from a chef. Moms was a defense attorney. Yeah, I know what you thinking, ironic right, but it works in my favor. If I ever need a lawyer, I have one and for free at that.

"What's up, ma, what you cooking in here smelling so good?"

"You know those twins of mine. They got to run out. One wants burgers and the other want spaghetti."

"Well, ma you and pops got 'em spoiled like that."

"Like you and Imani don't have a hand in spoiling them."

I had to admit between my parents, Imani, and myself they had everything they wanted plus more. All I could think to give them was money.

"So, ma what did you and pops get them for their birthday?"

"We got them that new iPhone they were asking for. The max or whatever it is."

"Damn ma, those phones are a G each."

"And, do you remember your sixtieth birthday? If I recall you wanted a car, right? A Challenger to be exact, and what did you get? Yeah, that's what I thought, hush mouth. If I want to spoil my babies, I damn sure will and best believe when you decide to give me some grandbabies, they gone be the same way."

"Well, you can wait on that cause I strap up every time."

"You better be strapping up from the way I hear you round the city slanging dick."

"That's cause the ladies love me."

"Get out my kitchen, boy."

"Yeah, yeah, where's everybody at?"

"Your brother and your sisters are out by the pool with Brianna."

"Damn, Bri's out there? That girl is annoying. I done told her I don't want her lil young self, but she won't give up. It looks like I'm gone have to hurt her feelings."

"Leave that girl alone boy, and go see your dad. He has been talking nonstop about that damn trip to Charlotte."

"Oh yeah, it's about that time."

"Umm, keep my husband out them damn strip clubs down there. The only stripper he needs is me."

"Dang ma, you bout to ruin the entire trip."

"Kase, don't make me slice y'all tires before you leave."

"Dang ok, ma. Where's pops at?"

"You know where he's at. He's in that man cave as he calls it."

Although we lived in DC, my pops was the biggest Carolina Panthers fan ever. He turned the basement into his very own Carolina man cave. I'm talking Panthers everything— chair covers, posters, pool tables the works. I even got him personalized Panthers shot glasses for his fifty-third birthday. My pops was an old-fashioned country nigga. Even though he lived in the city, he was Carolina born and raised. I admired my pops from coming from nothing to becoming a world-renowned heart surgeon. He worked his ass off to make sure my siblings and I had the best, and I respected him for that.

"Pops, what's your old ass in here doing."

"I got your old, lil nigga. I can still beat your ass. Don't let the age fool ya."

"Whatever old man, you ready for this trip?"

"Of course, I am, son. It's the Panthers home opener, and they're playing them whack ass Cowboys."

"Well, I'm trying to see some of them Carolina strippers, the best part of my trip."

"You better not be saying that around ya mama. She's already on my ass about it."

"Hell yeah, she mentioned it just now."

"Shit, you know your mama is a nut case."

"You're hell, pops."

"How's school going son? It will be December before you know it. You ready to walk that stage?"

"Yeah pops, I'm ready."

"Well, you don't seem ready. Son, is everything ok?"

"Yeah pops, everything is good. I'm ready."

"You have no idea how proud your mother and I are."

"Thanks, pops. Let me go and hand the twins their birthday money. I can't stay long. I got something to do tonight."

"Between you and Imani, those damn twins are spoiled as hell."

Talking to my pops about school was a very awkward conversation, although I was graduating in December with my Masters in Business Management, I still choose to sell drugs. It was the adrenaline that I felt when I was running the streets. I didn't plan to run the streets forever, but let's be honest. Once you're in there, you never really escape that life.

This upcoming trip was more than just a yearly trip with my dad. It was also a business trip. See, I was the connect for the Carolinas being that I had family down south. Because both of my parents are from down south, DJ trusted me to run the product down south. See little did most know, DJ was taking over the entire east coast. Even though Big L wasn't ready to give it all up to DJ, he was still making moves that would solidify his status as a kingpin. DJ was my boy no doubt, but lately, stepping down has been on my mind. Getting this sports bar off the ground is something that I always wanted to do. The next few weeks would be crucial for me.

"What's up y'all?"

"Hey, Kase with yo sexy ass."

"What's up, Bri?"

"Shit you and me, but you playing."

"Nah, I'm not playing. You not ready for a real nigga."

"Where's my sister?"

"Right here, Kase."

Imani walked up behind me looking just like our mother. I promise I would go to war behind my little sisters. I just prayed they didn't end up with no fuck nigga that would break their heart. I wasn't too worried about Imani like I was with Marie. Imani was focused on school, and she hardly went out, but my baby sister was still in high school and was starting to feel herself. You could tell by the way she dressed and acted. I had a plan too, but that shit to ease if I needed to. I had no problem showing my ass.

"Imani, what's up sis? Tell your friend she is not ready for me."

"I tried to tell her you ain't nothing but a hoe, but she doesn't listen."

"Nah sis I'm far from a hoe."

I always wondered what my sister had in common with Brianna, but they were best friends, so I didn't fuck with Bri. Although she was sexy as fuck, I couldn't do it. She was messy, and in my line of work, I couldn't deal with a messy female. I'd mess around and blow a bitch's brains out.

"I'm about to be out tho, so I'll holla at ya later. I gotta head on back to campus."

Of course, I wasn't headed back to the school. I had a lil shorty name Rhonda I was scooping up. Baby was fine, and I wanted to see what that mouth do. Fuck it. What Kaya don't know won't hurt her.

IMANI

"**M**ommy, Bri and I are headed out. I will back in a few days to take Marie shopping like a promised her."

"Ok baby, do you girls have plans tonight?"

"Not me, I have midterms coming up."

"What about you, Brianna?"

"I don't yet, Mrs. Peters. I also have midterms."

"Y'all should enjoy your weekends. Both of you girls are smart, so I know these midterms are nothing to either one of you."

"I know, mommy. I'm just trying to stay focused."

"And it's nothing wrong with that baby, but don't let life pass you by. Get out and enjoy yourself. You are nineteen and beautiful, baby girl."

"Paulette, you leave my baby alone. If she wants to stay home and study, then that's perfectly fine. She'll have plenty of time to go out or whatever it is once she finishes medical school," I heard my daddy tell my mother as he came down upstairs, from his man cave.

I was a daddy's girl to heart. In my eyes, my daddy could do no wrong, and as far as I know, he never did. My daddy showed me the way a man should treat a woman, which is probably the reason I was the way I was about men. I was accustomed to the way a man should treat a woman, so I refused to settle for just anybody. My daddy was not just my daddy, but also my personal doctor. See, I was premature and born with an enlarged heart. I had my first heart surgery at the age of three, which my father performed. His colleagues didn't think I would live to see the age of three, but my dad wasn't having that, and I'm still here at nineteen, so My father was very overprotected of me, all of us honestly.

"Marion, stop babying that girl and let her grow up. She is almost twenty, and she needs to get out and find her a good man so that I can have some grandbabies before I die or get too old to play with them.

"Ok, it's time to go. Mommy and daddy, I will see y'all later. Let's go, Bri."

"You don't have to leave baby girl. Ya mama is just hell-bent on having grandbabies. To be honest, I'm surprised your brother doesn't have about five different baby mamas floating around DC."

"That makes the two of us, daddy. What he needs to do is stop putting Kaya through the stuff he puts her through. If he doesn't want her, then let her go.

"Well, she needs to leave him then."

"Mom, when she tries to leave, Kase be about to have a damn heart attack like his whole world is coming to an end. Kase needs to grow the hell up and stop trying to be everybody's man.

"Leave my baby alone. She's probably out there doing her own thing too."

"Ok mommy, I'll see you later. I had to laugh at my mother. In her mind, Kase was perfect, when that was a fucking lie. My brother was one of the biggest man whores in DC.

"Imani, you know your mother is right. You need to get out more and enjoy life. Let's go to the club tonight. We haven't been to the club in a while."

"Brianna, we just went to a party last night."

"And that was last night. Tonight is a whole other night, and last night you just refused to have fun."

"I had fun Brianna; honestly I did."

"Imani, let's be serious. You didn't have fun, but the way you were staring at ole boy had you feeling some type of way, and you wanted him didn't you?"

"First of all, I wasn't feeling anyway type of way, and secondly, he was with someone, so I was far from his mind."

"Imani, wake up baby. The way he was staring at you, that man wanted you, and if he was with whoever she was, she wasn't on his mind."

I didn't bother to tell Bri that I saw him come back and pick whoever she was up. I must admit our eye contact was very intense. I could feel myself getting moist just by the way he stared at me. *Damn, he was fine.* Maybe it was time I let my guard down and try to meet someone. Someone more my speed cause he was definitely out of my league.

"Imani, are you listening to me?" I heard Brianna say.

"Yeah, what did you say?'

"I said let's go to the club tonight and just unwind before midterms. Please, Imani. I don't want to go by myself, and you know I don't fuck with a lot of bitches like that." Brianna knew I couldn't tell her no when she made her puppy dog face.

"Ugh, fine Bri, we'll go. Just meet at my house later. Right now I need to go to the library."

"Thank you, best friend. I love you."

"I love you too." Bri and I made plans to meet back at my place later that night, but right now, I was headed to school. If I was going out tonight, then I had to study extra hard today.

I took my time driving to school, and I kept getting flashbacks of the guy from the party, I didn't even know his name, but I found myself thinking about him. He seemed like the type that would break your heart, so I didn't know why he was on my mind, but he was so sexy. I made it to Howard's main campus in about twenty minutes and headed straight for the library. I had to get my head in my books soon.

"What's up Imani how have you been?"

"Oh hey Aaron, I'm good and yourself?"

"Good still waiting on my dinner date you promised me."

"Umm, yeah we can do that after midterms."

"You have been saying that since last midterms. I thought you enjoyed the last time we were together. I mean the way you were moaning when I was eating that pussy, I figured you would want some more. Maybe you'll let me sample that pussy this time. "

"Aaron, after midterms are over, I will go out with you."

"Ok Imani, I'm gone hold you to that."

"Bye Aaron."

Aaron and I messed around on a few occasions. We never had sex, but we did give each other oral sex. His head game was good, but sex was out of the question. I might take him up on his offer. I've known Aaron for about six years, and we have always had a great relationship. We ended up messing around the first time after a long night of studying and drinking. Aaron was very handsome, but we didn't have that connection that I was looking for from a man, especially if it would be with the man I planned to lose my virginity to.

I had to get my mind right, and the only way to do that would be to get my ass in the library, put my headphones on, and just let the music take over while I bury my head in a book. I made to the library and thankfully, it was not crowded. I pulled out my laptop and put my Apple air pods in my ears. I choose a little Boyz II Men to zone out to while I studied for midterms.

***

I was completely zoned out when I realized that it was almost nine o'clock, the library would be closing soon, and I was meeting Bri at eleven. I packed up, headed out of the library, and went straight to my car. I was going to have fun tonight. Fuck, why not enjoy life.

"Imani, what are you doing out so late?"

"Dang Aaron, you scared me."

"I'm sorry I didn't mean to scare you. I was coming from the gym, and I saw you headed to your car."

"It's ok. I was just leaving the library."

"This late, do you have plans tonight?"

"Yeah, Bri and I are going to the club just to unwind before midterms."

"The club, why the club when you can chill with me? These clubs ain't nothing but wanna be thugs and shit, that ain't your type of crowd, Mani."

"How do you know the type of crowd I like, Aaron?"

"Listen, Imani. I wasn't trying to offend you. You just don't seem like the ratchet club type."

"And I'm not Aaron. Just because I choose to go out to a club with my best friend doesn't make me the ratchet club type as you call it, and I find that very offensive. Maybe you need to choose your words a little better before you judge the next female, now you have a good night, Aaron."

I walked off and left his ass standing there with his mouth open looking really dumb. I don't know what has gotten into Aaron, but I would keep distant for a while. I headed to my apartment ready to hopefully enjoy my night.

DARIUS

"*T*his ain't no models or the bottles in the club R&B song. Girl, this that look me in my eyes, while you ride R&B song."

Trey Songz had to be one of my favorite artists. I sang along to Trey as I drove to one of my trap houses. I was serious about taking over from my pops. I was already making major moves on my own without him, so I was ready, and with this new Cuban connect, shit was about to be love. I was destined for that money and power shit. Even when I was a little nigga, I was running shit and demanded respect. My parents taught me at a young age that nothing in life is given to you, you have to go out there and earn that shit no matter what it is you choose to do. Whether it's selling drugs, flipping burgers, or what the fuck ever, be the best at the shit. My pops worked hard to get where he is, and that nigga will go down as a legend, and that's the shit I want.

I called Zay to meet me at the spot to help count up this money. I didn't trust a money counter. I needed my shit counted by hand and documented. I was the nigga that was serious about my money.

"What's good, playboy?"

"Ain't shit, headed over to Destiny to count this money."

"That's what's up. I need to hit up my barber. My shit is looking fucked right about now."

"That's cool, but what's the move tonight?"

"Shit, we can hit up Onyx, pop some bottles, and find some fine ass hoes to fuck with for the night."

"I told you, nigga. I don't fuck with hoes. I fuck with women."

"Whatever Darius, you trying to hit the club or not?"

"Gone head with that shit Darius, and fuck yeah we can go, just be ready by midnight."

"Nigga, I'll be ready."

"Aight, my nigga."

"Aight peace."

Once I made it to the trap, it was business as usual. I checked my surroundings and made sure I was strapped. In my line of work, you could never be too careful. You never knew when some lil nigga was going to grow some balls and try you, and I didn't mind putting that heat to work if needed. They had me fucked if they thought they would catch me slipping, fuck that.

I saw that the homie Marcus was at the trap. Shit, that was good. The more help we have, the better to get this money counted up. A nigga was hungry and trying to get some good soul food.

"Marc, what's up my nigga?"

"Ain't shit DJ, What's good with you boy?"

"Ain't shit my nigga, how's the business looking?"

"You know business is always booming around these parts."

"That's what I like to hear."

Marcus was the homie from way back. We grew up in the same neighborhood up until my pops moved us from DC to Maryland. We lost contact for a while, but once I started moving wait throughout the DMV, we linked back up, and it was business from there on out.

"How long you been out here?"

"Shit, I have been out here for a lil minute."

That's what's up too. Shit good?

Shit's good, but there is one thing I meant to run by you and Zay."

"And what is that?"

"That nigga Kase has been acting strange. Maybe it's just me, but he seems like he ain't tryin' to put in no work."

"What you mean, Marc?

"I hit that nigga line, to come through and help count this money, cause I know how you feel about who counting this shit up, that nigga was like *'Nah ain't you DJ and Zay right hand. You count that shit. I got other shit to handle that doesn't involve counting money for DJ.'"*

"That nigga said that?"

"Yeah, I was like whatever. I can handle the shit myself."

"Look, DJ. I ain't trying to be no snitch bitch, but I'm just saying watch that nigga closely."

"Good looking nigga, I will keep my eyes open."

"Other than that shit what y'all niggas getting into tonight?"

"Shit, gone hit the club scene trying to find my future queen. You sliding through?"

"Nah, I got a lil honey dip around the way, and I'm trying to see what that bitch's mouth do."

"Keep fucking with these bitches and both of your baby mamas' gone fuck you up and shoot your dick off."

"Baby mama 1 and 2 just mad cause I ain't fucking them."

"You wild, man."

"You know me, I'm young, fine, got plenty of money, and I love pussy. The hoes can't stay off me."

"You sound just like Zay, man."

It's true my dude. You just gotta live life to the fullest."

"Yeah ok, but shit come fuck with us at the club tonight. You know we doing it big VIP style, man."

"I'll see what's up, DJ."

"Shit let's count this shit cause a nigga is hungry as fuck."

***

It took about three hours to count the money. I was serious about not staying there for long. Shit, a nigga needed food asap. I dapped up Marcus and headed to a local steak and potatoes shop around the way from my spot. I was ready to get the fuck home and tear this steak and eggs up. I drove through the city just contemplating life. I often wondered if I would be in the game if my moms was still living. She was hard on a nigga growing up. Even while she was sick, she stayed on my ass about doing the right thing and making an honest living. She knew what my father did for a living, but she never wanted that for me. *Damn, what is my pops doing here?*

I saw pops car parked at my spot when I pulled up. I could only imagine what this was about. I took my time getting out just to get my thoughts together when dealing with my pops. I was never the one to disrespect either of my parents, but It was time for pops to let me take over. He would always be a legend, but it was time to allow his prince to shine.

"What's up, pops?"

"There you are, son."

"What brings you here pops?"

What I can't come see my one and only son?"

"Yeah right, old man. You think you are fooling somebody, but you got one of them young girls waiting on you."

"No not tonight, son. I just came by to see how my boy was doing."

"Whatever pops. When you gone settle down and find you a nice lady your age instead of fucking with these young thots out here in these streets?"

"There is not a woman in this world who could take your mother's place, so there is no need to waste my time looking."

My mother Elizabeth died from breast cancer when I was ten. That was one of the hardest times of my young life. I began to act out, so that's when my father decided to enroll me in basketball, but I was never the type to take orders from anyone, so basketball didn't work out. That's when my father decided to move them us from DC when I was twelve. At first, the move was very hard on me— new surroundings, new school, and new people. Eventually, I met Zay, and the rest is history.

"Nah son not tonight, I actually came over to see how things were running since securing the deal with Emmanuel."

"Shit, work is running smoothly, you know like clockwork. The product is legit, and it's moving."

"That's what I like to hear. You know I am handing this all solely to you soon. Do you think you ready, son?"

"Yeah pops, my team is A-1, our little routine is smooth, and my workers know what's up when it comes to my money."

"That's what I like to hear, I trust Emmanuel, so I know you in good hands."

"Pops, it sounds like you're taking my advice and stepping all the way down."

"Nah it ain't nothing like that young blood. I'm just making sure my boy is straight."

"Ight, you hungry, pops? I got some steak and eggs here if you hungry, and I still got some time to kill before I meet Zay at the club."

"Nah I got to head on out. I need to go check on these barbershops, get a haircut, and find me a little cutie to wine and dine for the night."

"Ight pops; I knew it you can't help yourself. We'll chop it soon."

"Ok, son."

After pops left, I had a lot of thinking to do. Hella moves needed to be made, and I had to move pops out the way. This money was calling my fucking name, and I was going for it. I needed to hit Zay up cause this shit Marc put on about Kase was fucking with me. Was that nigga really feeling like that? Of so then we needed to have a conversation. I needed to see if that nigga had an issue that we needed to resolve.

XAVIER BENNET

ll you fucking do is stay in the damn street with fucking DJ and all them hoes."

"Jada, what the fuck are you bitching about, man damn?"

"I'm talking about how you never want to come spend time with your damn daughter."

"What the fuck do you mean? I was just with my daughter the other day."

"What the fuck is one day, Xavier?"

"Look, man, I will come get Mya on Saturday, god damn."

"What come and get her and take her to your mother's house?"

"Look, Jada, like I said I will get Mya Sunday, now bye."

On God, I couldn't deal with all that damn bitching today. That damn girl is gone make me kill her ass. Here I was at twenty dealing with this bullshit every day. Sometimes I wished I had strapped up with fucking with Jada's dumb, hoe ass. She was the main reason I didn't trust bitches in the first damn place. My baby mama was the fucking devil, and I swear if it weren't for my baby, her ass would be dead and fucking buried.

When I first met Jada, shit was cool. Our vibe was straight, and she was sexy as fuck with a body that would make any nigga wanna wife her up. We were still in school when we met, and I was still a young nigga in these streets. About a year into our relationship is when DJ and I started making a name for ourselves and making a lil bit of paper. Soon after, Jada got pregnant with my baby. Man, that shit was scary. At first here I was just coming up and bringing a life into this world, but I ain't no bitch, so I made sure to handle all of my responsibilities. I moved Jada in our first house and kept shit running for us. All the fuck she had to do was take care of my baby. When my baby was born, everything was perfect. I was a young nigga with a family, and I made my baby a promise that she would never need anything as long as I was breathing. For the first six months after Kamya was born, shit was still good with us— at least I thought so. I know some females go through a depression stage after the birth of a child, but damn, I didn't expect Jada ass to be so fucking grimy.

"Damn Jada, this is some good pussy."

"Yes Nick, daddy right there, daddy!"

"This is my pussy. Damn, I'm bout to nut, Jada."

"Ahhhhh I'm cumming daddy, I'm cumming!"

"What the fuck, Jada? In my fucking house, hoe."

"Nigga, who the fuck are you?"

"Who the fuck am I?" I'm the nigga that's going to be the reason your hoe ass mama has to buy a new black dress!"

POW! POW! POW!

"Ahhhhhh Oh My God, what did you do to my husband? Niiiiccckkkkk!"

"Your husband, so you nasty ass bitch, you liked watching your husband fuck another bitch?" Watch that shit in hell with that nigga!"

POW! POW! POW!

Just like that, the woman was dead.

"Oh my god, Zay, what did you do? I'm so sorry, oh my god, I'm so sorry."

"Bitch you sorry, you fucking sorry, the fuck you sorry for? Getting caught or your fucking bitch ass boyfriend and his wife losing their life? Get the fuck out my house before I put a bullet in your head just like I did these two muthafuckas."

"Zay, please just talk to me. I'm sorry baby, please."

Never one to hit a female, I grabbed Jada by her neck and pushed her up against the wall.

"You better be fucking glad for my daughter cause had it not been for Kamya, I would kill your dumb ass and cut up your fucking hoe ass body and bury it in the middle of nowhere. Now get your shit and get the fuck out of my house before I fucking kill you, Jada."

"Zay, listen to me please."

"Listen to what bitch? You in my house, fucking another man in my fucking bed while his stupid ass hoe ass wife watches the shit, so what the fuck can you possibly say to me?"

"Zay, I was alone. You were never here for me, I'm sorry. I was here with Mya all day alone, Zay. I needed you."

"Are you fucking serious right now? I'm never here? You were alone? What the fuck do you think I'm doing out here. I am running these fucking streets every fucking night securing the bag so that you and my daughter can have the best, so fucking dismiss me with that shit. Now I suggest you take your hoeing ass downstairs and get the fuck out before I put a hole in your head, and don't even think about taking my daughter with you."

"Zay, please, no please."

"GET THE FUCK OUT NOW!"

I had to get myself together. That shit still fucked me up. That was the first time I had ever caught a body— shit two in one night. I believe that shit is what turned my heart cold. These days only two females have my heart— my baby and my mama. Other than that, fuck these hoes.

"Zay, do you hear me talking to you?"

"Jada what the fuck do you want, I told you I would come get her on Saturday."

"What is one day Xavier, one day, is that all she is worth to you is one day of your time? It's bad enough that when you get Mya, she spends the entire day with your mama. You don't spend no time with Mya."

"Man, look. I will come by today and see Mya so that you can stop fucking bitching."

"I wouldn't have to bitch if you would be a man and help me with her sometimes. Money isn't always what the child needs."

"Look, man. I said I was coming chill the fuck out."

"Hmm whatever, Zay."

I swear I couldn't keep dealing with her bitching. Maybe I can just shoot her ass and get Mya a nanny. Who the fuck is that calling my phone?

"What's up?"

"What up, boy?"

"Man, ain't shit. I just hung up with Jada's stank pussy ass."

"Oh word, shit is good with my goddaughter, right?"

"Yeah, Mya's good. Jada's bitching about I don't get her enough, but that bitch just wants an excuse to call my phone."

"Yeah that's what it sounds like to me but check it. You know I was down at Destiny earlier today talking to Marcus, and he told me Kase has been moving and acting kind of funny."

"What you mean?"

"I don't know. Marcus was telling me he asked him to help him count this money up and Kase was like he's got better shit to do than count money for me."

"The fuck is that supposed to mean?"

"Man, I don't know but have you noticed that nigga acting funny?"

"Nah, I haven't noticed anything."

"Me either, I'm not going to say shit, but I will keep my eyes open."

"Hell yeah, that doesn't sound like Kase tho."

"No, but that nigga had been talking a lot about that sports bar shit, especially when he graduates."

"That is true, but I don't think that man is moving recklessly like that tho."

"Shit DJ, I would say something to the nigga."

Nah, not yet, I wanna observe some shit first."

"I wouldn't wait too long. You know he makes that trip down south in a few days."

"Yeah, I might just wait until he comes back."

"Aight DJ, just don't let that shit get too far."

Nah Zay, you know that's not how I handle shit."

Aight well get up, I need to go see my baby and give Jada's dumb ass some money."

"Man, I don't see how the fuck you deal with her ass. I would have been put a bullet in her ass."

"Shit had it not been for Kamya I would. She keeps fucking with me, and I will be a single father."

"Ight Zay, go handle your business. I will holla at your tonight."

I was dead fucking serious about being a single father. Jada took that being my baby mama shit as a free meal ticket. I was about to kill that shit.

Pulling up to Jada's spot, I could feel my blood boiling. She and her hoe ass sister were sitting on the porch, and I hated them bitches just as much as I hated Jada's dumb ass.

"There go you baby daddy," I heard he oldest sister Tiana say.

"And what the fuck that got to do with you, Tiana?"

"Zay, don't come here with that bullshit, I don't have time for it. You coming to get Mya?"

"Just because you out here with your hoe ass sisters don't think I won't knock you the fuck out. You better watch your fucking mouth and didn't I tell you I would get her tomorrow. I came by to give you some money, dumb ass."

"Umm hmm, and you better not have her around none of your nasty ass hoes."

"I will have her around whoever the fuck I want to have her around. Shit, I'll fuck around and have Mya a stepmother."

"I wish the fuck you would, Zay."

"Keep fucking with me Jada and watch. Now you out here with these hoes, where my baby at?"

"Fuck you, Xavier. Where else would she be besides in the house?"

"Nope, you can't anymore. Go fuck Nick in hell. Yeah, that's what I thought. Let me go see my baby before I catch a charge in broad daylight."

Jada always had a way to pull me out of character, but I didn't give a fuck what I said to her. She deserved it plus more.

"Dada, dada!"

"There goes my baby, give daddy kiss. Daddy's coming to get you soon." I talked to my baby as if she knew what I was saying when all she did was smile. That smile was everything to me, and also the reason her mama was still in her life.

"Zay, can I talk to you?"

"No."

"Zay, please."

"Jada, what do you want? All I came to do was see my baby, not hold any type of conversation with yo ass."

"Zay, please just talk to me."

"You got two minutes."

"Zay I am sorry, can we please work things out, I miss you and Mya misses you. I swear on everything I am sorry. Please, why can't you forgive me? I talk a lot of shit Zay, but I know I fucked up, and I am damn sorry. I just want my family back."

"Jada, keep your sorry. You made the ultimate fuck up, and I will never forgive you. The only reason I come around here is for Mya, not you, so get whatever fantasy you got about us out your head cause I will.

"Here, I will be back to get her tomorrow and have her looking nice. I am taking her shopping and make sure you pack her a bag. She may stay a few nights with me. I gotta go."

I left Jada standing there looking dumb as fuck. The fuck I look like fucking with her again? Fuck that and fuck her sour pussy ass. I would be a dumb nigga to go back to that trifling bitch, nah I'm good. I wasn't gonna let Jada put me in a fucked mood. I was ready to hit the club with my boys and get fucked up. It was about that time for me to get fly for the hoes.

IMANI

“**D**amn this club is packed. It looks like we picked the right one tonight, everybody and they mama at the club. It's definitely my type of party.”

Bri was right. This was her type of crowd. I would have much rather stay home, but it was hard to tell Bri no. Call me a sucker but seeing Brianna happy made me happy. We were finally able to find a parking spot and made our way to the club. Thankfully the line to get in wasn't that long.

“God damn lil mama. Damn you fine.”

“Imani, girl, the niggas are out tonight.” She was right it was a lot of guys out and a lot of good-looking guys at that.

Bri was looking sexy as fuck in an off the shoulder black and red shorts romper and a pair of six-inch black, red bottom stiletto pumps. We were without a doubt killing the game tonight. The club was packed wall to wall, and even the bar area was crowded. The club was a double level, so the upper level was VIP, and it was not as crowded as the main level, but it was jumping. I saw a few people from school, but the majority of the people were new to me. I didn't get out much, so of course, I wouldn't know a lot of people, unlike Brianna who seemed to know everyone that came up to her.

Finally making our way through the club, our first stop was the bar. I needed my usual pineapple juice and vodka. I made Bri a promise that I would try and have a good time and why not start with a drink.

"What are you drinking, Imani?"

"Pineapple juice and vodka, you should know that Bri."

"Of course, well order me a Henny and Coke. I'm about to hit this dance floor. I feel a twerk session coming on."

The bar had since thinned out a little just enough for me to order our drinks. I ordered my pineapple juice and vodka along with the Henny and Coke and took a seat. Brianna was tearing that dance floor up, she was definitely enjoying herself, and we had only been here maybe fifteen minutes. I sat there at the bar nursing my drink.

"Don't I know you?" I heard someone say.

"I don't think so."

"You go to Howard, right?"

"Yeah, I do."

"Well, that's where I know you from. Well, I don't know you, but I have seen you around campus. Your Kassem's sister, right?"

"Yes, Imani, and your name is?

"Jamarion, but you can call me Jay."

"Nice to meet you, Jay."

"Same here, Imani."

"You don't come here too often, do you, Imani?"

"Why would you say that, Jay?"

"Because you look tense like you are forcing yourself to have fun."

"I wouldn't say I was forcing myself. I only came out because my best friend wanted to come."

"Got you, so you are forcing yourself." I laughed because he was telling the truth.

"You should really try harder Imani, tell you what you wanna dance?"

"Jay, no, I am not a dancer."

"Come on. You look to fine to be sitting here baby girl."

"Ok, maybe later."

"Ok Imani, I'm gone hold you to that."

"Ok, I'll be here."

Why was I being so shy? He seemed like a nice guy. I really had to loosen up when it came to men. I just knew what I wanted when it came to the opposite sex. I had a fear of falling for someone and getting my heart broken, and it just being a continuous cycle. I didn't want that. I wanted stability and unconditional love. I want to come home to a family. Most would say at my age that I shouldn't worry about that and just live life. Maybe I should.

I thought about going after Jay, but someone else caught my attention. Just like last time, our eyes locked and contact was intense. *Damn, this man is fine.* He was in VIP surrounded by beautiful woman, and just like last time, he was probably here with someone.

"Thanks for the drink, Imani," Brianna snapped me out of my thoughts.

"You're welcome, Bri."

"What's wrong Mani, you look nervous."

"Nah, I'm good."

"Sure, so who was that you were talking to? Yeah, you didn't think I saw did you?"

"Bri, whatever he was someone that recognized me from school, and he knows Kase."

"Ok and, stop being so lame Imani and talk to that nigga. He is obviously trying to holla at you. How do you expect to find someone if you push everybody off?'"

Deep down I knew she was right. I just needed to loosen up. I decided not to tell Bri who I saw in the VIP area. I was not his type, so why worry about it. I saw Jay make his way back to the bar, and I decided to just go for it if he approached me again.

"Come on, Mani. Let's get on this dance floor and show these hoes out."

As soon as we got to the floor "Tempo" by Chris Brown came on. I was a huge Breezy fan, so whenever I heard Breezy, it was on. Bri and I hit the dance floor like were the only two out there. I was starting to loosen up little a enjoy myself. I saw Jay walking up towards me, and I Just continued to dance to Breezy.

"I see you decided to let loose."

"Yeah, why not enjoy myself right."

"Ummm, glad you decided to cause I am enjoying the view."

"Oh, are you really?"

"Hell yeah."

Jay and I continued to dance as Ella Mai's "Boo'd Up" came on. Something told me to look up, and I noticed the guy from the party coming my way. He was headed right towards Jay and I. He said something to Jay that made him look at me and walk away.

"Now that he is gone let a real nigga talk to you. I'm Darius, but you can call me DJ."

"Imani, what did you say to him?"

"I told him you needed a real nigga in your life, and to step off."

"What makes you think that you're what I need in my life? You don't know me."

"I don't know you yet, but I can tell by the way you kept staring at me that you wanted to get to know me, so why don't you come on up to my section in VIP so that we can get to know each other?"

I came here with my best friend, and I don't want to leave her."

"Shit, she can come too, as long as you say yes."

"Ok let me talk to her."

I walked over to where Bri was, and she looked like she was having the time of her life. I didn't want to disturb her, but I didn't want to leave her and she not know where I am.

"Imani, what's up girl? I saw you working up on ole boy. Get it, girl."

"Yeah, I was."

"What you mean, what happened?"

"Well, look who is over there waiting on me to go up to VIP."

"Who, bitch?"

"Just look over there, Bri."

"Oh shit, Imani is that ole boy from the party, the real fine one?"

"Yes, that's Darius or DJ."

"Oh shit y'all exchanging names and shit, so what the fuck happened with Jay?"

"Bri, I don't even know. One minute Jay and I were dancing, Darius came up and said something to him, and Jay just left, and now Darius wants me to go up to VIP with him."

"So why the fuck are you standing here? Go with him girl."

"I wanted to let you know where I was first, and I wanted you to come with me."

"Shit Imani, you ain't saying nothing but a word, let's go." Brianna and I walked back over to where DJ was, and he was texting away at his phone.

"DJ, this is my best friend Brianna, Brianna this DJ."

"Nice to meet you, Brianna."

"Same here DJ, but you can call me Bri."

"Ok, Bri. Y'all ladies ready?"

"Yeah."

I didn't know what I was getting myself into, but I would just go with it, besides I had my best friend with me. Bri and I along with DJ made our way to VIP. I couldn't help but notice the stares and smirks from other females who tried to get into VIP, but of course, it didn't faze me. I was used to other females beefing with me for nothing at all. However, this time was different, and I knew exactly why.

"Your girlfriends are getting mad."

"I don't have a girlfriend... yet."

"Yet?"

"Yep."

DJ was perfect. The way he licked his lips, the way he held his blunt between his lips, and even the way he pronounced his words. His smile was contagious. His teeth were perfectly straight, which made him even sexier. I also noticed the bulge that was trying to escape his gray joggers that he was wearing. Just looking at DJ had me ready to lose my virginity. I couldn't help but stare at him.

"Imani."

"What's up, Bri?"

"Before we go up, walk with me to the ladies room."

"Alright."

"I'll be back," I whispered to DJ.

"Ok," DJ whispered back.

DJ's scent had me moist and weak in the knees. Lord, I pray that I didn't lose my balance and fall face first as I walked away. Bri and I made it to the ladies room and thankfully I didn't make a fool of myself by falling, but he had my knees weak.

"Girl, that nigga is fine, you better scoop that nigga up because there are plenty of bitches in this club that would love to be up there right now."

"Bri, I barely know him, and we haven't even had a conversation yet."

"Well, get to know him, Mani."

"I am so nervous, Brianna. I don't know what to say to him, and I don't want to sound like a lame by saying the wrong thing."

"Imani, just be you baby girl, the amazing Imani you have always been. The way you have been eye fucking that nigga, I can see you like him, and obviously he likes you too. Give that fine ass man some pussy before I do."

"Brianna!"

"No, I am just fucking with you Imani."

"Oh my god, Bri."

"What? Come on. Let's go back to your man."

"He is not my man."

"Girl, you know you want that nigga, stop playing."

"He is fine Bri, and girl that smile."

"Got you wet, huh?"

"Go to hell, Bri."

"Go ahead back up to VIP. I'm gonna stay down here. I can't be with you every step of the way in life, Imani. You got this just be you. If any shit pops off just call me, and I'm up there. I saw how those hoes were looking, but I promise you they don't want no smoke with me. Love you, now go."

I headed back to the VIP area while Brianna stayed on the dance floor. It was just too crowded out there for me. The floor was packed, and I wasn't built for that, I also wanted to get back to DJ. I was really feeling him and didn't want to lose that connection. I never got like this about a man, especially one I just met. It would take me a while to warm up to someone but with DJ it just flowed, and I was loving it.

I made it back up the steps and DJ was right on me. He introduced me to his friends who I now knew as Zay and Marcus. I can recall a few times Kase talking about some dude named Zay, but this is DC, so everybody got a nickname.

"Nice to meet you all."

"Nice to meet you," the one named Zay said. The one I knew as Marcus was too busy on his phone to notice anything else.

"Where is your friend, Imani?"

"She went back down to the main level. This is her type of crowd. Tonight was all her idea to come out."

"Well remind me to thank her later for making you come out tonight, so I guess she made you come out the night of the party as well, huh."

"Yeah, she did."

Damn, he was saying all the right things to me, I just kept paying that I didn't say something lame and sound like an idiot around. Was this really happening? Was I about to let my guard down and try and get to know someone? Maybe this is what I needed, but in the back of my mind, I just knew he had females everywhere. He just seemed like the type. DJ was fine, and he knew he was fine. Just as the thought left my mind, I heard someone yelling from the entrance of the VIP section.

DARIUS

When I saw Imani on the dance floor with Jay ole bitch ass, I knew it was time for me to make my move. She was far too beautiful to be with that lame ass Jay. I knew Jay from around the way. He was a local trap boy who tried to make a come up but was too fucking loose at the tongue, so I knew he couldn't be on my team. I knew for a fact he was trying to spit that weak ass game to Imani, so I had to go and rescue baby girl. I looked at Zay, and he knew exactly what I was thinking. We both knew Jay was too much of a pussy to try anything, but I made sure I was strapped before making my move, just in case he wanted to grow some balls.

I made my way down to the main level of the club and walked directly to Jay and baby girl. I know she saw me and cause we locked eyes. I figured I would take the smart approach and just tell Jay what he wanted to hear.

"Yo my nigga, we can do this the easy way or hard way. Step away from shorty, and I will put you on my team, if not I'll just make you disappear, and you know I can and will. She's outta yo league, my nigga."

Seeing Jay sweat I knew he wouldn't try me. Just like I thought his bitch ass just walked away. I invited Imani up to VIP because I wanted to get to know her. She wouldn't come without her friend, so I said fuck and told her to bring the friend too. Her friend who introduced herself as Bri was sexy as fuck too, but she didn't have anything on Imani. Imani had a natural beauty, and you can tell she didn't need makeup. She was just beautiful.

"Fellas, this is Imani and Brianna, ladies this is Zay and Marcus."

"Nice to meet you."

Damn her voice was sexy. I don't know what it is about this girl, but it was something. She looked like she was nervous, but she had no reason to be nervous.

"Come over here with me Imani and have a seat."

"Ok, thank you."

"You don't have to be scared, Imani. I won't bite you."

"It's not that. I just see that your girlfriends are getting a little upset."

"I don't have any girlfriends… yet."

"What made you come to the main level and stop my dance with Jay?"

"Because Imani, I've been watching you since you walked through the door. When I saw you walk in, my eyes followed your every move, so when I saw you talking to bitch ass Jay, I knew I had to step to you. I missed my chance at the party, and I didn't want to let the second chance pass me by."

"I don't think you missed your chance. I believe you were with someone if I'm not mistaken."

"Nah she wasn't anybody special, just a chick from around the way."

"I don't know if you can tell our not, but I don't usually go out. I only came out because Bri forced me to come out."

"Well remind me to thank her for forcing you to come out."

"Damn DJ, I see why you can't answer your damn phone. You up here hoeing around."

"Janae, what the fuck, and who the fuck let you up here?"

"Who let me up, oh you too good to have me in your section now?"

"Janae, get the fuck out. Don't make me embarrass you up here. You know how the fuck I get down, so just fucking go, man."

"You know what fuck you, DJ. You ain't shit but a dog anyway. You better be careful all he gone do is fuck you."

"Yo, get her the fuck out."

I didn't know where the fuck Janae came from or who let her up. She knew how I got down, so I don't know why she chose to fuck with me like I wouldn't jack her ass up in the club in front of everyone. Here I was telling Imani that Janae didn't mean shit to me, and here she go acting like we fucking married and shit. I had to make a move quick.

"Damn, I am sorry about that Imani, I didn't know she was gonna flip like that. Shit, I didn't even know she was in the club tonight."

It's cool. If that's your girlfriend, I can leave. I don't want any issues between you two."

"Trust me, Imani. She is not my girlfriend. As I told you I don't have a girlfriend, Janae is just someone I used to fuck with, that's it. Tell you what. It's a little crowded in here. Let's go outside where we can talk alone and try this again."

"Alright, we can go."

I led Imani out of the club, gently placing my hand on the small of her back again. This was a gesture that I just had to do. I felt as if he needed to protect her for some reason. We walked out the private entrance to the club to avoid all of the partygoers. I led Imani to my car, and opened the passenger side door and let Imani get in. I quickly ran to the driver's side and got in. I decided on some Trey Songz to play. I knew some Trey would set the mood.

"Pinch me if I'm dreamin', as a matter of fact, I take that back. Let me lay there, inside of your love. Listening to your heartbeat, there ain't no feeling, better than feeling on your body. Girl, don't you move a muscle. Girl, I just wanna touch you."

Trey Songz "It Would Be You" played gently through the system in DJ's car.

"I have never heard this song before, and I know Trey Songz."
Imani giggled

"Then you don't know Trigga if you never heard this song."

"Trust me I know about Trey. He is one of my favorite singers."

"Oh really, what's one of your favorite albums by him."

"One of my favorites was definitely his last album the *Tremaine* album. The first six songs got me through a lot of late night study sessions."

"You not lying. That album was dope, and his *Trigga* album was fire also."

"Yeah, it was. I have been a Trey Songz fan since he had braids and a fitted."

"Well, other than you being a huge Trey Songz fan, tell me more about yourself, Imani."

"What would you like to know?'"

"Well, start by telling me what your name means."

"My name is Swahili, and it means faith."

"Is there a reason behind your name?"

"Actually there is, I was born prematurely with an enlarged heart. My parents said when they found out about my condition they leaned on their faith, so they named me Imani. The doctors didn't expect me to live beyond the age of three, but my parents didn't want to hear that."

"Damn, that's deep. So are you good now as far as your heart?"

"I still have to see a doctor once a month for routine check-ups, and of course, I have to take medication, but on the bright side, my dad is a heart surgeon, so I guess I am in good hands. He's the one that did my heart surgery."

"Oh word, so I take it your dad is your Doctor?"

"Yeah, he wouldn't have it any other way."

"Can you blame him, I would definitely protect you."

I noticed that every time I would compliment Imani, she would lower her head and hide her smile, something that I would have to get her to stop doing.

"You really shouldn't hide your smile."

"What do you mean?"

"Every time I compliment you, you put your head down, but I can tell that you are blushing. See, you're doing it now."

"It's a habit I guess."

"You shouldn't. Your smile is too beautiful to hide."

"I should get going. I'm pretty sure Bri is looking for me."

"Just text her and let her know you in good hands, I'm not ready to end the night unless you go other plans, then I understand."

"No I don't have other plans, I just don't want her to worry, but I will text her and let her know that I'm good."

I watched as Imani took her iPhone out of her purse and unlocked it. I noticed that her password was 821505. I didn't want her to see that I was watching, so I pulled out my phone as well. I sent a quick text to Zay to let him know I was good and to keep Bri entertained. I didn't need her coming out looking for Imani. As I said she was in good hands and the night was still young.

***

Imani and I talked for the next few hours. I learned a lot about her, and it was dope having a real conversation with a female without the subject of money or what I could do for them. The vibe was dope, and I wanted more.

"Damn, I didn't know it was so late the club probably closing in few."

"You know what they say time flies when you having fun."

"You're right. I need to text Bri and see if she is ready. I promised my baby sister that I would take her shopping tomorrow."

"Yeah, I got some moves to make myself in the morning so you can go, but not before we exchange numbers."

I unlocked my phone and handed it to Imani so that she could lock her number in. I decided to call the number she put in my phone so that she could save mine as well. As soon as I stored Imani's number in my phone, I saw Zay and Brianna coming out of the club's private entrance.

Imani, are you ready to go cause these heels are doing a number on my feet right now? The club is all fun and games until your dogs start hurting. Fuck around, and I'm gonna start bringing Jordan's in this bitch."

"Yes Brianna, I'm ready. Good night, DJ."

I watched as Imani and Bri walked off. I knew then that I would be hitting Imani up very soon. I wanted to know so much more about her. The story she told me about her being born prematurely with a heart condition was deep. Her name fit her so well, but I knew it was more to this beautiful woman that I just had to know.

XAVIER

"Why the fuck you look like you all in love, nigga?"

"Man fuck you, Zay. Let's ride."

"Ole pussy whipped ass nigga, meet at my spot."

The entire drive to my spot, I couldn't get Brianna off my mind. She was sexy as fuck, but I knew the type of female she was, and I wasn't ready for all that, but I wouldn't mind fucking her a few times. Shit, I'd even keep her on standby for those late nights after the club. When DJ texted me and told me to keep her occupied so that he could chill with lil mama for a while, I stepped to her cause she was sexy as fuck. I brought her back up to VIP with me, and she even smoked with me, but that lap dance she did took the cake. I swear she had me ready to bend her over the couch.

About twenty minutes past before DJ and myself arrived at my condo. My spot was definitely a bachelor pad. I had everything from a mini bar to a stripper pole in my living room.

"I still don't know why you got a stripper pole."

"Because I love strippers, and they're freakier after they work."

"You a straight clown, Zay."

"Indeed, my nigga."

"Yo, tell your girl I'm trying to fuck her friend."

"Man, I'm not telling her that shit and have her thinking I'm some fuck nigga like yo ass."

"Look, I ain't no fuck nigga. I'm just not about that lovey-dovey shit no more. That shit has been dead since Jada's ass."

"You gone have to let that shit go one day, not every female is like Jada's ass."

"Nigga, you one to talk, I have seen you with your share of bitches on many occasions."

"Yeah, I fucked my share, but I think it's time to settle that shit down and find my queen so that we can rule these streets together."

"DJ, I hope you don't think that Imani is the one. She is not your type, man. I mean yeah she is beautiful, but she not about that street life. She is outta your league, man.

"Maybe that's what I need man, someone who is not in the game. I need someone who just wants me to come home and cuddle and shit, not worry about how much money I plan to give her to go shopping or some shit like that."

"So, how do you know Imani isn't like that? I know you didn't get all that from a few hours in the car at the club."

"Actually, I got a lot from those few hours. She's a fucking medical student at Howard for one, my nigga. Financially she ain't gone need a nigga, so we just gone make money together."

"How you know she interested in a street nigga, maybe another DOCTOR is her type. All I'm saying DJ is don't get so wrapped in that fairytale love shit that you don't see the bitch playing you right under your nose. These hoes are scandalous. They look innocent and shit until it's too late, and they done fuck your world up, and you catching bodies because you caught feelings."

"Who the fuck said anything about a damn fairytale, the fuck is you talking about? Your baby mama got you fucked, my nigga."

"Fuck that bitch. I'm just being real DJ. That love shit will cause niggas to flip the fuck out."

"You on some other shit right now, so I'm bout to ride, my nigga, I'll holla at your crazy ass later."

"Alright you old Babyface begging ass, I'll holla at you tomorrow. "

After DJ left, I poured myself another shot of Hennessey. I thought about calling up one of my many late night freaks but decided not to. For some reason, I couldn't get my mind off of Brianna. We had exchanged numbers in the club, but I wasn't ready to hit her up just yet. It was something about her that had me intrigued. She was young, but she acted so much more mature. I decided to call it a night. I had planned to get my baby girl tomorrow and take her shopping. Kamaya was the most important person in my life, and I knew without a doubt that she was the reason Jada was still living.

After that night, I swore I would never let another female hurt me the way Jada did, and that's why I did woman the way that I did them— I fuck em' and leave em. I knew DJ was right about trying to settle down. I just wasn't ready. I would have to take a very special woman to change my mind and my mindset. I was focused on my money and making sure that Kamaya was good. Being a father changed me in a lot of ways. I now had to move smarter. I couldn't be reckless anymore, and that stood for my woman too. If I ever allowed another woman to come into my life, she would have to understand that my baby will always come first, and if that was a problem, then she could step.

IMANI

I sat on the side of my bed in nothing but a towel. I had just gotten out the shower. It was Saturday, and I planned to take Marie shopping and spend some time with her. Marie would be headed to college soon, and I wanted to spend as much time with her as possible. Even though she was coming to Howard, she would be living her own life, so I made sure to spend as much time with her as I could.

Grabbing my Moonlight Path body lotion from my favorite store Bath and Body Works, I took a long look at myself in the mirror. People have always complimented me on how beautiful I was, but deep down I just considered myself to be average. My natural hair was the one thing that I loved about myself. I was passionate about my hair, and it took me years to finally perfect my hair. I heard my phone ringing, and I knew that could only be one of two people Brianna, or Marie. Looking at my phone, it was neither one.

DJ: *Good morning beautiful.*

Me: *Good morning DJ.*

DJ: *I know you said you were taking your sister shopping, but do you have plans tonight?*

Me: *No, I didn't have any plans for tonight other than studying.*

DJ: *Let me take you out to dinner tonight. I'll make reservations and everything.*

Me: *Umm, yeah we can do that. I'm looking forward to it.*

DJ: *Same here just text me your location, and I'll pick you up around nine, is that cool?*

Me: *Yeah, nine is good. I'll text you the address.*

DJ: *Aight bet, see ya later, Imani.*

Me: *See ya later DJ.*

I sat on the side of my bed and just looked at the text between DJ and me wondering what just happen. DJ was not the typical guy that I would talk to let alone date, but it was just something about him that had me telling him yes to a dinner date, but it also a little scary. He was fine, but his bad boy persona is what turned me on. I knew that tonight would be different from any other date that I have ever been on. I contemplated canceling the date. I didn't know anything about DJ other than what he chose to tell me last night. I didn't even know what he did for a living. He wasn't flashy like the guys that sold drugs. He didn't drive a flashy car like a Lamborghini or nothing like that, and he didn't wear a lot of jewelry. What if he just wanted sex? I had witnessed one female damn near going off on him in the club, how many more were there? What did he do? Where is he from? These were all questions that ran through my mind.

I definitely saw something in DJ, but there was also something mysterious about him. He was so nice and gentle at the club, and the way he would place his hand on my back and guide me felt like he was protecting me, but from what. I never felt this before, and it scared me a little bit. This date was definitely going to be different, and I would need some advice from Bri, but I didn't want to call her. This had to been done face to face. After my planned shopping trip with Marie, I needed to do a pop up at my best friend's place. I was ready to step out and do something different, and maybe DJ was my different that I just had to go with. I couldn't back out, and I didn't think I wanted to.

I knew today would be busy, so I decided to put on something comfortable, so I chose a black and gold Nike sweat suit with my black and gold Air Max would have to do. My baby sister was the queen off shopping, and we would often spend up to five or six hours in the mall. So I knew today wouldn't be any different.

***

"OMG Mani, this dress is bomb. I got to have it!"

"No, that dress is too revealing, and you know mommy and daddy would have a fit if they saw that dress on you, girl."

"Mani, come on, it's 2018. Mommy and daddy don't have to know everything."

"What? Let me find out you hiding and sneaking things from mommy and daddy."

"I've been doing it for years."

"Oh my god, whatever Marie, let's go."

We spent another two hours in the mall shopping. I couldn't believe how beautiful my little sister was. I just prayed she stayed on the right path and continued with school and not get boy crazy. Marie was very developed for her age. She honestly didn't look like she was sixteen but more like twenty. I wasn't going to act like I didn't notice every time her phone would get a text message that she would get this goofy smile on her face, so I knew it was some lil boy that had her nose wide open.

"Let's go, Mani. I'm hungry."

"Finally, girl, I thought you were going to never be done."

"Whatever sis, you act like you got plans tonight when we both know all you're going to do is go home and study."

"Well, baby sis, if you must know. I have a dinner date tonight."

"Stop lying, Imani."

No need to lie baby sis, I know how to have fun."

"Sure, ok, Mani. Anyway, let's hit up Cheesecake Factory, a chick is hungry."

We grabbed our bags, which was about five bags each. One thing about the Peters' sisters was we knew how to shop, and fashion was a big hobby for Marie. She would often dress her friends for special events or dates. She even helped to coordinate the outfits for my senior prom, which won us best dressed.

Driving to the restaurant, I kept thinking about DJ. *That damn boy is so fine,* I thought to myself while biting my lower lip.

"What you over there thinking about?"

"Don't worry about that, baby sis."

"So tell me about him, Imani."

"There is nothing to tell yet. This is our first date."

"Well is he fine fine, or is he your type of fine?"

"Marie he is fine fine. It's just something about him."

"Let me find out you lusting over him. I need to meet this mystery guy that has my sister all googly-eyed."

"Why don't you tell me who is texting you and got that goofy grin on your face, Marie?"

"Oh, that's Omari, girl. He is sexy as hell, Mani. He is a star football player, runs track, and lifts weights. He asked for my number a few weeks ago, and we been texting, but it's nothing serious yet. I hope he hurries and asks me out."

"Omari huh, just watch out for those popular ones, Marie. You know what they want."

"Shit, sis Omari can and will probably get it that boy is sexy."

"Enough about Omari, how is school going, Marie?"

"It's going pretty good this semester. I've got straight A's across the board like always. It's that twin brother of mine that you need to be asking about school. It would be a miracle if he went to school five days a week."

"What do you mean, where the hell is he going when y'all leave for school and have you told mommy and daddy or Kase for that matter?"

"No, I haven't told anyone, and I have no idea where he is going. Major is going to do what he wants so why waste my time. You can tell mommy, daddy, and Kase if you want to, but I wash my hands with him. Honestly, I think he is running the streets with those weak ass dope boys around school."

"Our parents along with Kase and me make sure y'all have whatever it is y'all want and need. The hell he gotta sell drugs for? I mean where would he even get that idea is beyond me, but I am going to have a talk with him and have Kase there as well to get to the bottom of this."

I pulled out my phone and sent a text to my baby brother letting him know that I needed to talk to him. I then sent one to Kaseem with the same message.

"I just sent his ass a message, and he better be home when I take you home."

"Get your stuff and let's go, Marie."

"But I'm still eating."

"Get a to-go box. I will meet you at the car, and hurry up."

I grabbed my things and headed outside to the car. I was really in my feelings about Major. My parents did the best they could for all four of us, so why would Major have the need to sell drugs. I didn't understand, but I was surely going to get to the bottom of it, and skipping school was also unacceptable. Both of them knew how our parents felt about education. Major was always the rebellious child, even as a little boy he just did what he wanted, but I never thought that there would be a possibility of him running the streets.

It was a thirty-minute drive back to our parents, and to my surprise, both of my brothers were there, but I didn't see either of my parents' cars in the driveway, which was good.

"What's up, Imani?"

"Don't what's up Imani me, Major. What is this I hear about you skipping school and supposedly running the streets?'

"The fuck is she talking about, Major?" Kaseem asked, "You selling drugs, Major?"

"Damn, y'all acting like y'all my damn parents. The hell is y'all problem?"

"It's not about us being your parents but us wanting what's best for you. Major, you have no reason to be in the streets. Kase and I, along with mommy and daddy, make sure you Marie have everything y'all want and need, so please tell me why you feel the need to sell drugs if that's what you're doing?

"Man, whatever Imani. I'm good, and as for you, Marie. Mind your fucking business. I bet you ain't tell Imani how you around the school being a thot, did you?"

"Boy, fuck you. I ain't no damn thot. I've only been with one person so go to hell, Major."

"Everybody shut the fuck up!" Kase yelled. "First of all Marie the fuck you doin' fucking at your age? What the hell is going on with y'all? Y'all wildin' and shit. And Major whatever it is you think you're doing get the fuck out now, cause once you get in that shit deep, it's hell to get out."

"And how would you know that Kaseem?" Major asked.

"Because lil nigga, I know, just get the fuck out that shit, and who the fuck you supposed to be running for anyway, huh?"

"Man that's none of your business, now both of y'all can go back to Howard and don't worry about me, I'm good believe that. Y'all come jumping down my damn throat from what Marie told y'all, but she ain't tell y'all what the fuck she doing."

"And what is she doing?" Kase and I asked at the same time.

"Being a damn hoe, trying fuck every nigga in school."

"Boy, how the fuck would you know what I'm doing in school when you never in school?"

"Let me get out of here. I can't begin to imagine what the two of you are thinking, and how would mommy and daddy feel about this y'all acting like we weren't raised by two who worked their ass off to make sure we had what we needed and wanted. I am highly disappointed in both of you. Kase, I will call you later."

I grabbed my keys and headed back to my car. I had to clear her head before tonight. My siblings were acting as if they weren't raised right. I didn't understand why they needed to act out. Maybe I needed to spend more time with both of them individually to see what was going on. Maybe it was something at home, but our parents were good parents, so I just didn't know. I needed to talk to Brianna, so I headed right over to her dorm.

KASSEM

"*Fuck the frail shit, cause when my coke comes in, they gotta use the scale that they weigh the wales with. Carsons on the jeep but Gotti made the prototype. Hoped you get the picture but you can't just photo light. Determined niggas make it, kicking down the door and we burning niggas naked.*"

I drove through the city listening to Jadakiss "We Gone Make". That shit with my younger siblings had me fucked up. I had no idea who the hell Major was supposedly running drugs for. I knew it wasn't for us, so who the fuck was it. I needed to find that shit out and ASAP. I knew what the game was like and I wanted out, and I didn't want that for my little brother. Shit, he was only sixteen. It's bad enough I didn't know when I would have the time to get info on his supplier because I had this damn Carolina trip coming up next weekend.

I loved making money, no doubt, but recently I wanted more to get this sports bar off the ground. I had always been book smart and believe it or not math was one of my of my favorite subjects. I always dreamed about owning a chain of sports bars along the east coast, which is what DJ, Zay, and I always talked about, but recently the only thing that mattered to them was taking over the game from DJ's father Big L. I just didn't have the passion for it anymore. I promised myself that after this last Carolina run, I was stepping down to focus on my bar. I planned to have a meeting with the guys as soon as I got back to discuss the plans, but right now, I was headed to my baby

Kaya's house. Kaya was my main lady and would one day be my wife. We've been off and on for over three years. I loved Kaya, but I also loved pussy, so I still cheated from time to time.

I arrived at Kaya's spot about twenty minutes later. I had to admit although I laced my girl's pockets, Kaya was doing pretty well for herself. She worked at the local Bank of America and also did hair and makeup on the side. She would usually do makeup and hair only for special occasions but one day dreamed of having her own shop.

"Kaya, where you at bae?"

"I'm in the kitchen."

"Damn it smells good in here what you cooking up for daddy?"

"Some lasagna and hot wings."

"Damn, you gone let daddy taste that pussy for dessert?"

"No Kase, move."

"Damn, what the fuck is your problem? And please don't start all that bitching cause I will get the fuck up and leave."

"You can fucking leave cause I am tired of your lil hoes always in my inbox about how good you fuck them."

"Oh my god, Kaya what the fuck are you talking about?

"You know what. Let me just show you the latest message, Let's see. This is from Rhoda last night. *"Damn, your nigga got some good dick. I see why you be ready to fight bitches over him. Let him know he can sample this pussy more whenever he's ready."*

"Yeah don't get quiet now, Kase. Were you quiet last night sampling Rhonda's pussy?"

"Kaya I don't know what you talking about, I don't know a fucking Rhonda. You know these hoes will do anything to get you to stop fucking with me. How many times do I have to tell you, I'm not fucking nobody but you. I love you, Kaya. You know that you will be my wife one day, I promise you."

"I swear Kase I don't want to fuck with you no more. Three years and I am still going through the same shit with you, If you don't want me, just let me fucking go so that I can find someone who will appreciate me.

"Kaya, you must really want me to fuck somebody up, I told you if I see you with another nigga that it will be his blood on your hands cause I will blow his fucking brains out, so don't fuck with me. Now fix me something to eat please."

"Fix it your damn self."

Kaya stormed off and headed for the back of her condo. I felt like shit for the things I was putting Kaya through, but I just couldn't imagine another nigga fucking her, and I was dead ass serious about it, but sometimes temptation gets the best of me. I really did love the fuck out of Kaya and one day wanted her to be my wife and have my kids. I knew I needed to let her go until I was truly ready to settle down and commit to just her.

I fixed my food and went into the living room to watch *SportsCenter*. I would allow Kaya to calm down a little before I went to try to talk to her. After about an hour, I figured she had calmed down a little, and we could talk, or I could just fuck real good.

"Kaya, baby, where you at? We need to talk, bae."

I walked in Kaya's room, and she was laid across the bed in nothing but a tank shirt and boy shorts. I could tell she had just gotten out of the shower since I smelled her Moonlight Path body wash and lotion. I knew that scent very well because that's all Imani wore. Looking at Kaya had me instantly bricking up in my pants. Kaya was fine. She stood at five feet five with a slim waist, and her ass was fat. She had her sandy brown hair pulled into a messy bun. The little butterfly tattoo that was on her shoulder blade was one of the sexiest things on her body, and that was her spot.

Damn, I could see that pussy through her boy shorts. I stripped down and got in the bed with Kaya. I pulled her close and started kissing on her shoulder right where her tattoo was. I slowly moved my hands inside Kaya's shorts. Finding her clit, I began to massage it gently. With my other hand, I grabbed Kaya's breasts and began to make circles around her nipples. She began to moan and started to squirm. I flipped Kaya on her back and took off her shorts, getting right between her legs. I placed two fingers in Kaya's pussy.

"Damn ma you tight and wet just like I like it."

"Kaseem," Kaya moaned out.

"Didn't daddy tell you he was gone eat this pussy for dessert?"

"Mmmmm...Kaseem."

I kissed down Kaya's stomach and down both of her thighs until I found her sweet spot. That damn lotion smelled so good on her skin. I used my tongue to make small circles around her clit, and the more I sucked on that pussy, the more her clit jumped.

"You gone give daddy's pussy away?"

"Nooooooo Kase!

"I'm gone ask you again and say it right this time. You gone give daddy's pussy away?"

"No, daddy."

"That's better."

I continued my oral assault on Kaya until she came twice back to back. I then used my tongue to lick up all of Kaya's juices. I stood up and removed my boxers. Kaya sat up on her elbows and looked on as all ten inches of my dick was freed from my boxers. I reached in Kaya's nightstand, grabbed a condom, and handed it to her. Kaya got of bed and got on her knees. I knew what time it was, and I was ready. Kaya wet her lips and placed the tip of my dick in her mouth. Slowly she put more in her mouth until she had as much as she could fill her mouth up. I threw my head back and let off a soft moan. Kaya's head game was definitely the truth.

"Damn bae, suck that shit! Bend over and let daddy slide up in that pussy."

Kaya climbed on the bed on all fours, giving her back the perfect arch that she knew I loved. I slid on the condom, sliding behind Kaya. I gently slid the head of my dick inside her going slowly and deeper until I had all ten inches inside.

"Damn ma, your pussy is tight. Throw that ass back for daddy."

"Kaseem, ahhhh Kaseem!"

"Fuck Kaya, fuck mmmm!"

"Turn that ass over."

Kaya laid on her back just like I told her to. Placing both of Kaya's legs in the crook of my arms, I slid deeply back inside Kaya's pussy. I then slowly stroked Kaya. The love faces she made had me getting hard with each stroke. Damn, I wasn't ready to nut just yet. I pulled out of Kaya and put my head between her legs and begin sucking on Kaya's pussy like I was hungry, making sure not to miss any of it.

"Don't you run from me."

"Kaseem, I'm cumin', I'm cumin'!"

"Cum for daddy, just like that,"

"Kaseeeeemmmm!!!!"

"Open up and let daddy slide back in that pussy."

I slid back in Kaya this time a little harder, and with each stroke, Kaya dug deeper into my back.

"Damn, I love this pussy, and I love you."

"Kaseem, I love you. God, I love you."

After a few more minutes, we came together. We just laid there in each other's arm, staring at each other, neither one of us knowing what to say, but both deep in thought.

"When you gone stop hurting me, Kase?"

"Kaya, I'm not doing shit how many times do I have to tell you that shit. I told you these bitches would do anything to fuck with you, baby."

"I don't believe you, and I can't keep doing this Kase. If you're not doing shit then why are we still using condoms after three years of fucking? Why won't you stay with me like you used to, and when you do your fucking phone is constantly going the fuck off? Don't lay up here and tell me you not cheating on me because its bullshit, and I am tired of your lies, Kaseem. I'm tired of sitting here waiting to see if you are gone call me or at least spend time with me. I love you, Kase, lord knows I do, but I love myself too, so until you ready to be with just me make this your last time coming, and I mean it."

"Kaya, I'm gone leave because I can tell you are in your feelings right now, and I am tired of having to explain myself to you every fuckin' day."

"No Kase you no longer have to explain yourself to me. I'm done."

Kaya grabbed her clothes and headed to the bathroom. I laid on the bed recalling the words Kaya had just told me, and something deep inside told me that Kaya was serious this time. I couldn't, and I wouldn't let that shit end like that, fuck that. Just the thought of another man with Kaya pissed me off. I grabbed my clothes and went into Kaya's guest bathroom to clean myself up. I really had to get my shit together and make it right with Kaya. I really couldn't lose her.

DARIUS

I sat on my couch paying *2K18,* but my mind wasn't completely on the game. My thoughts drifted from Imani to work. Deep down I had my doubts about taking over from my father. That nigga is a fucking legend in this game. Mentally I was ready, but emotionally I had my slight doubts. A knock on my door pulled me from my thoughts.

"Who the fuck is that at my door?"

I looked at my cell phone to check the time and saw that I had two missed calls and texts from Kase telling me that he was on his way over to talk. Looking at the time and the time of the missed messages, that had to be Kase at the door, but to be on the safe side, I grabbed his gun before opening the door.

"What's good, Kase?"

"Damn nigga, the fuck you in here doing? I called you like three times. If you got company, I could come back."

"Nah, you good, I was just in here playing some *2K.* Come get your ass beat right quick."

"Boy you know you cannot beat me in no damn *2K,* fuck round and get your feelings hurt, but nah I'm not staying long."

"Alright, come on in."

Before sitting down to chop it up with Kase, I checked my phone to see if Imani texted me. Here it was almost six o'clock, and lil mama still hadn't sent me her address. I hope that shit with Janae didn't scare her off. Speaking of Janae, I see she texted me though.

Janae: *I miss you DJ, and I am sorry about last night. Can we talk and I can make it up to you? You know I hate to see you with another bitch. Why the fuck you try to play me?*

Me: *I told you I'm not with all that drama and we not together why is that so hard to get through your head?*

I hit send on the text and put my phone back in my pocket.

"What's good with you Kase, what brings you by?"

"What's the deal with these Cubans, and when is this shit gone be official?"

"I'm not quite sure. I still got few ends to tie up with Emmanuel and his crew."

"Where you coming from, the trap?"

"Shit, I'm just leaving Kaya's house, and she's on some bullshit talking bout she gone find somebody else and shit. I told her she must want blood on her hands cause I wouldn't hesitate to pop that nigga if I saw her with him."

"Shit, it sounds like Kaya's ass ain't playing with you no more."

"Kaya will be alright. She knows what it is and how I am. She better not be out there on some single shit like she don't have a man."

"Nigga you stupid. You keep right on fucking with Kaya, but when is the last time you been down to the trap? That nigga Marcus be putting in that work at the spot.

"I ain't gone lie, other than the other night when we had our lil meeting it's been a minute since I been down there. With school and shit, and this trip coming up, I haven't been there like that."

"Oh, word?"

"Shit, but that's why I'm here now because I need to re-up before this trip to Charlotte this weekend. Last I talked to my cousin he said that shit was moving like crazy."

"Yeah man, shit is good. I got to admit I had my doubts at first only because I am not big on change, but shit is legit, and Emmanuel has kept his part of the deal."

"Facts, shit is looking real good. I'm just ready to turn this shit legit and get this sports bar opened."

"Here you go with that sports bar shit. It's gone happen just not when we anticipated. We gotta get this takeover with pops running like clockwork first."

"Yeah, I hear you DJ, but I'm about to bounce. I'll holla at you before I leave."

"Bet."

I was starting to believe that shit Marcus told me about Kase was true. I pray that nigga wasn't on no funny shit. I would hate to put a bullet to that nigga's head. I heard my phone go off and I prayed it wasn't Janae's ass. I wasn't in the mood to deal with her ass right now. Thank God it was Imani texting me her address.

Imani: *1824 7th St SW APT 201*

Me: *I was beginning to think you were gonna stand me up.*

Imani: *No, I wouldn't do that.*

Me: *Good, I will be there @ nine.*

I couldn't help but smile at my phone. For a minute, I thought she was going to stand a nigga up. I was praying that shit with Janae's ass didn't scare her up. The last thing I needed was for her to think that I was some fuck boy who just wanted to fuck her and leave. I was dead ass about Kase. If that nigga were on some fuck shit and fucking with my money, then I would have no choice but to leave that nigga bleeding. My whole crew knew how I got down about my money. That's the one thing to get your life ended for good no questions asked.

I had to clear my head for my date with Imani tonight. I wanted to dig deep into lil mama tonight. Once I had her, I wasn't letting her go, and I meant that. I could see myself coming home to shorty and just hearing about her day and shit. Yeah, I was into that lovey-dovey shit. I learned that shit from my pops. True he was a legend in the streets, but at home, he was that nigga. My pops would always cook dinner for my mom, run her bubble baths, and would always come home with flowers and shit. Without him knowing it he taught me how to treat a woman. He taught me how to keep a woman happy. You know the old saying "happy wife happy life" , yeah that shit was true. I can't recall one time when my folks argued or fought. If they did, they hid that shit from me very well. My ole lady always had a smile on her face. That's what I want. I woman I am happy to come home to. No one should dread coming home to their spouse. I'm pretty sure Imani is green to this street life, and I want to keep her as far away as possible.

BRIANNA SUMMERS

L ast night was so fucking epic. I really cut all the way the fuck up. Although Imani left me to be with DJ's fine ass, I still made the best of the night. That damn Zay that's is a sexy ass man, and I felt everything he was working with when I gave him that lap dance. I don't know if it was the Hennesy or the weed, but I was feeling that. When he stepped to me, I was a little surprised. I wasn't expecting him to step to me the way he did, but the nigga was smooth with his shit tho. I definitely didn't think I would end up in VIP with him and dancing for his ass at that. We did end up exchanging numbers, but I need to do a little investigating before I used the number. I'm not no gold digger or no shit like that. By investigating I mean checking his social media accounts to see how many women he follow, and how many pictures he is commenting on, you know shit like that.

All that would have to wait this was Saturday night, and I would be spending in my dorm room. Usually, I partied Thursday-Sunday, but I had midterms coming up, and if I wanted to keep my scholarship, I had to maintain a "B" average overall. I wasn't failing or no shit like that, but I had to maintain the average I had, and that meant passing all midterms with nothing less than a B, and in order to do that, I had to sacrifice the club life for the remainder of the weekend. I didn't have rich parents like Imani, so I needed to keep that full scholarship so that I could stay in school. Tonight and tomorrow would be nothing but trap music and my laptop. I didn't have a roommate, so I could play my music as loud as I wanted.

Although I technically lived on campus, I had my own suite that came with my scholarship. The shit was lit for real. Everything was paid for plus Wi-Fi and cable. I made a little extra money by tutoring some of the struggling students when I had the time, but mostly I would just call my dad for some cash.

I got my studying kit ready to begin my weekend session when someone knocked on my door. Not really in the mood to be bothered, I instantly got an attitude. When I looked out the door, I saw it was Imani, and she looked upset. Imani was one of the only people that I would drop anything for.

"Hey, best friend. What brings you here, why you look so mad, and what's wrong?"

"Them damn twins are gone make me kill them. I swear I'm just gone kill they ass both of them and Kase's ass too and this time he ain't did shit, but I'ma kill his ass too and just be a whole single child out here."

"Oh my god Imani, what is going on?" I asked my best friend while laughing,

"This shit ain't funny, Bri. I'm dead ass serious, bruh."

"Ok, ok I'm sorry, Imani. What's wrong?"

"So apparently Major's out here trying to be a kingpin, skipping school to run the streets and Marie's in school thotting and fucking at sixteen. The fuck wrong with these kids?"

"Imani, what the fuck are you talking about? Ain't no damn way that Marie's out here fucking and you not."

"Bri, really?"

"Ok, I'm sorry. Tell me what's going on."

I listened as my best friend ran down the events of the day, I felt bad for Imani. I didn't know what to say. Unlike Imani, I didn't have any siblings close to my age. I had two younger brothers from my father's second marriage, but they were five and six, so I didn't know the words to say to her. All I could do was listen and let her vent.

"Damn boo, so what are you going to do?" I asked my best friend.

"I don't know, but I don't want to take this negative energy with me tonight on my date."

"Wait, bitch, what date?"

"DJ asked me to dinner tonight, and I said yes."

"So you weren't going to tell me about your date?"

"Bri, I was going to tell you, but I got caught up with my damn siblings.

"Imani, you need to tell your parents what's going on."

"I don't want to involve my parents and have them all stressed out. I was hoping Kase, and I could knock some sense into them, but

Kase has been on some other shit lately, so I don't know what his issue is. I feel like I am the one trying to keep this family straight.

"Look, Imani. That is your problem. You worry too much about others and not yourself. I am pretty sure the situation with the twins is not as horrific as you're making it out to be, and if Marie is fucking, then she is doing a hell of a lot better than her big sister that's for sure. Right now, what you need to do is go home make yourself a drink and get ready for your date. Clear your head so that you can have a conversation with your siblings and your parents because they need to be involved in whatever it is Major and Marie got going on, and as far as Kase is involved, Kase is a grown ass man. Concentrate on Imani for once, please.

"I know you're right. I just want the best for them all three of them, so it's hard not to worry, Brianna. I honestly don't want to take this negativity with me tonight. I'm just going to pray about it for now.

"That's exactly what you should do. Now I would love for you to stay and gossip all night, but you got a date, and I have a weekend full of studying, so I am kicking you out and make sure you send me a picture of you when you get dressed. I love you, now bye."

"Damn Bri, are you sure you studying tonight? You kicking me out mighty fast. I think your ass is lying about studying, and you got someone coming over here. That's fine I get the point. I'm leaving."

"I wish I were lying, but you know I gotta keep my GPA up to keep this scholarship, now go."

Imani grabbed her keys and phone and headed for the door. I hugged my best friend, closed the door behind her, and got back to my bed so that I could begin this fun-filled weekend of studying. *This is going to be a long night, so I might as well get comfortable.*

***

After a few hours of studying, curiosity got the best of me. After hearing of Imani's date with DJ, I was curious about Zay, so I pulled out my iPhone and opened my Instagram account. I didn't know where to start, but I took a chance and pulled up Kase's Instagram account, I knew that nigga knew everybody in DC. I scrolled through his followers and after about ten minutes of scrolling, I didn't come up with anything, I was tempted just to give up and get back to studying, but then I saw that he followed DJ, which was the info I needed. I knew if Zay had Instagram then him and DJ would follow each other.

As soon as I clicked on DJ's profiles, I see Zay's picture. His profile picture was sexy as fuck. It was of him standing next to an all-black Dodge Challenger. He was wearing an all-black Nike sweatsuit with his hood over his head. The diamonds in his mouth and those beautiful gray eyes set the picture off. Thank God, his page wasn't private. I could look without following him. The first few pictures were just of him, but one picture caught my attention it was of him and a beautiful little girl. She looked to be about two years old. The caption of the picture caught my attention, *"The only girl who will ever have my heart"* with the hashtag daddy's girl.

Damn, he's got a kid. With kids came baby mama drama, and I wasn't built for all that. I knew first hand that a nigga can claim to not fuck with they baby mama, but yet they still fucking. I think that was my sign to keep my distance from Xavier Bennett.

Imani

I made it home around seven o'clock, and my nerves were really getting the best of me. I grabbed my keys, bags, and phone and stepped out my car and headed to my apartment. I made it up to my apartment and did the usual check around. I lived in a very secure apartment complex not too far from campus, but you could never be too careful, especially living alone. I decided just to set the mood for the night by lighting a few candles and putting on some music. I put on some Trey Songz as I got myself dressed. I decided on a black and gold dress I paired it with some black stiletto gladiator sandals. A matching black lace Victoria Secret bra and panty set finished the look.

I grabbed my Moonlight Path shower gel and lotion and headed to the bathroom. The water temperature was perfect and stepping in the water felt amazing and so relaxing. About fifteen minutes later, I was out of the shower. Using my Moonlight Path body lotion, I made sure to hit every spot of my body. Standing in nothing but my bra and panties, I just stared at myself in the mirror. I would always run my finger down the scar across my heart. I was thankful for my scar. It was a part of the reason I was so strong. I always knew my heartbeat for a purpose. I just had to find it.

I wanted to wear my hair straight tonight, so I took a few minutes to run my flat iron through my hair and give it a part down the middle. I didn't wear a lot of makeup, just a little highlighter and lip gloss. My diamond hoop earrings and my "I" chain finished my outfit off. I glanced at myself in the mirror, and I was very pleased with how the entire outfit came out. I took the picture to send to Bri, and then I decided to post it on Instagram and Snapchat with the caption *"Stepping out of my comfort zone tonight, wish me luck."*

As soon as I posted the picture, I got a text from DJ. It was now or never. I couldn't back out now.

DJ: *I'm outside, do you mind if I come up.*

Me: *Sure Apt B7.*

DJ: *On my way.*

Me: *Ok.*

I grabbed my phone and walked to the living so that I could let DJ in. The slight knock on the door let me know that he made it to my apartment. "Here goes nothing," I whispered aloud as I opened the door and almost lost my breath.

This time DJ was dressed more casual in a pair of black and gray True Religion distress jeans, a black Polo sweater that fit perfectly, and a pair of black Jordan 12's that looked like they were fresh out of the box. The waves in his hair would make any woman seasick. This man was just perfect.

"Come on in, and have a seat. I am almost done. I just have to grab my purse and keys."

"Take your time, no rush. We have all night."

"Didn't you make reservations?"

"Yes at 9:45 so we'll make it."

"Ok, well have a seat."

A few minutes later, I walked out of my bedroom, and I couldn't help but noticed the way DJ looked at me. The way he licked his lips had me slightly blushing. This man was the total package for sure.

"I'm ready, DJ."

"Damn, ok, beautiful. Let's ride."

I locked up my apartment and headed out with DJ. I said a slight prayer that everything went smoothly tonight and that I didn't embarrass myself. Boyz II Men played through DJ's car stereo, which really impressed me. I was one of the biggest Boyz II Men fans, and I can thank my mother for that because all she would play was Boyz II Men. I remember she even took me to a concert when I was twelve, so I was loving the music choice.

"So you live by yourself, Imani?"

"Yeah, it's closer to my school, and that's where I spend most of my time."

"Oh yeah, I thought the part of town looked familiar. I gotta a homeboy who goes to Howard."

"Really, so are you on campus often?"

"No nothing like that. I just been through this area a few times."

I was relieved knowing that he didn't visit campus often, I just knew how the females would flock to him if he did, but I wondered who his homeboy was that went to Howard. I was tempted to ask him, but I didn't want it to seem like I was being nosy or anything like that.

"What you thinking about over there, Imani?

"Oh nothing, I'm just enjoying the ride. Where are we going?"

"I made our reservations at this local steakhouse in the city."

"Ok sounds nice."

We rode for another twenty minutes until we arrived at our destination. DJ made reservations at this restaurant in the city. The restaurant wasn't a very big restaurant, but it had a nice outdoor eating area that looked over the city. Again, DJ had me impressed with his restaurant choice. Being the perfect gentleman, DJ opened the door for me to get out of the car. He placed his hand on the small of my back, the same gestor he did at the party. I felt secure with DJ.

We made it inside the restaurant, and we were seated immediately. The area we sat in was slightly dim, which made the atmosphere very romantic. I couldn't keep myself from staring at DJ. He looked so sexy sitting there looking at his menu.

"What are you drinking, Imani?"

"I'll just have a glass of water with lemon."

"You sure, they have vodka if I'm not mistaken. You did say that's your drink of choice."

"I did say that, but tonight I'm taking it easy. Water with lemon is fine."

"Have you been here before DJ?"

"Yeah, I've been here a few times."

"What's good on the menu?"

"I like the steak and potatoes with a side of steamed vegetables."

"The vegetables and potatoes sound good."

"What about the steak?"

"I actually don't eat steak. I know that's lame, right?"

"Why would I think that's lame, Imani? You like what you like, baby girl. I'm not gone fuck with you any differently because you don't like steak. You're not getting rid of me that easy baby girl."

"Who said I was trying to get rid of you?"

"Good, cause I'm not going anywhere."

Something about the way he said he wasn't going anywhere had butterflies in my stomach, and I couldn't keep from smiling at DJ. I felt like a schoolgirl with her first crush. DJ knew all this stuff about me, but I didn't know that much about him. I figured now would be the best time to inquire about Darius. I just didn't know where to start. Should I start with what he does? Or should I start by asking about his family? I didn't know where to start.

"Are you from DC, DJ?"

"I was born here but moved to Maryland after my mother died when I was ten, and then moved back once I graduated high school. My mother passed away from breast cancer, and I started showing out in school getting into fights and things, so my pops moved us to Maryland."

"I'm sorry to hear about your mother."

"It's ok. I don't remember much. I can remember her smile and her scent, but the one thing that never leaves me is the day she passed. I can still remember the last words that she told me before she closed her eyes forever. She told me she loved me and to make her proud."

"DJ, I'm so sorry. You don't have to talk about this subject if you don't want to."

"No why are you apologizing, Imani? You didn't do anything wrong. You didn't know, and that's why we're here right? We're getting to know more about each other, so you don't have anything to be sorry for. I don't mind talking about my ole lady. Although she has been gone so long, I still get in my feelings about her sometimes, especially when I think about my future."

"What about your future?"

"A family."

"I understand."

DJ and I talked for another hour while we sat and enjoyed our dinner. It was a little before midnight when we finally left. For some reason, I was starting to get nervous as we got closer to my apartment. I didn't want the night to end, so the thought of asking him to come up crossed my mind, but if he said no then I would feel some type of way. I decided just to swallow my fears and ask him if he wanted to come up for a while. I just hope he says yes. The drive to back to my place seemed a little shorter compared to the drive to the restaurant, probably due to the fear of having to end my night with him. I saw a sensitive side to DJ tonight when talking about his late mother. There was so much more I wanted to know. I just hoped he would accept my invite up to my apartment.

"DJ, would you like to come up for a while?"

"Yeah, I can do that."

I honestly was expecting him to tell me no, but thankfully he said yes. We made up to my apartment, and DJ and I walked in.

"You can have a seat, DJ. I'm going to go to the back and change. I have water in the kitchen so you can help yourself."

"Nah I'm good, I'll be here when you get back."

"You can turn the TV on. I will be back in a few."

I headed to my room to change into something more comfortable, I had no idea what might happen tonight, but I knew I wasn't ready for DJ to leave just yet. I heard my phone go off and noticed that I had an Instagram notification.

"I hope stepping outside your comfort zone was worth it." I couldn't help but blush at the message. I looked at the name and knew exactly who it was— PrinceofdaDMV.

I decided to slip on a pair of tights and a t-shirt to join DJ in the living room. Walking back into the living room, DJ was on his phone texting, and I became jealous for some reason. The thought of him texting another female had me slightly in my feelings, but I couldn't say anything cause he wasn't my man, but the way that I was feeling right now I wanted him to be my man.

"Damn, even dressed down, you're beautiful."

"Thank you."

"What have I told you about hiding that smile? Let me ask you a question, Imani. Why did you invite me up?"

"I wasn't ready for you to leave."

"Is that it, or is there something else you wanted. If it is, tell me."

"I want you DJ, but I'm scared."

"What are you afraid of Imani? I told you from day one I wouldn't hurt you."

"I have never been with a man sexually DJ. I'm a virgin, and I am afraid to lose my virginity to you. Feelings may get involved, and I don't want to be hurt."

"Imani, I already told you that I wouldn't hurt you. I promise you that, but if you decide to take it there with me tonight, then you're mine, I will protect you, but I won't share you with anyone else. I knew that night I saw you at the party that you would be mine and I meant that.

I nodded my head and allowed a slight tear to run down my face. DJ gently wiped the tears from my check, and slowly moved in to kiss my lips. His lips were so soft slowly caressing my lips. DJ released the kiss, and I watched as he slowly bit his bottom lip.

"Come with me, Imani." I nodded my head and followed DJ down the hall to my room. We walked into my room, and DJ closed the door and led me to the bed.

"Are you sure you're ready cause if you're not, let me know now. I won't feel any type of way, and we could just chill, but if you say yes, just remember what I told you. You're mine, and that pussy will be mine, so are ready?"

"Will it hurt?"

With a slight chuckle, DJ looked me in my eyes. "At first it will hurt but not for long."

"Ok, I'm ready."

DJ laid me on my back and gently began kissing me. With each kiss, his hands touched different parts of my body. He placed his hand on my breasts and began to caress each one gently.

"Strip," was all I heard from DJ's deep sensual voice.

I did as I was told and took off all my clothes just as DJ instructed me to do. I was completely naked as I laid back down on my bed and covered my breasts.

"Move your hands, don't hide anything from me." Again I did as I was told and watched as DJ stripped down to nothing but his Polo boxers.

He spread my legs and stared at my naked body. DJ gently caressed my pussy, paying close attention to each spot. He then got on his knees and placed soft kisses on each of my thighs

"Mmmm… DJ, that feels good! DJ, DJ, DJ I'm cumming!"

"Cum for me baby girl, I want all of it."

"Ahhhhhh, DJaaaaaaaa ahhhhhhh, don't stop please."

"There you go. Give it to me. Give me what I want."

My legs shook uncontrollably from the feeling that I was getting from DJ giving the best head I ever had.

"DJ, I'm ready. I want youuuuuuu, pleaseeee!"

DJ continued his oral pleasure for a few more minutes. DJ stood up and took off his boxers. I couldn't help but gasp at the size of DJ's dick. Brian had nothing on DJ; this man was blessed beyond.

Fear set in but I couldn't back out now. I wanted DJ and now was the time. He pulled a condom from his wallet and rolled it in his beautiful dick.

"It's gonna hurt when I put it in, but it won't hurt for long, just relax."

DJ kissed me and took his knee to spread my legs. He then took his hand to find my opening. Guiding himself inside of me, he applied just a little pressure. Tears ran down my face, and he kissed them away. The pain only lasted maybe three minutes, but it was all pleasure from there.

"Damn, this pussy feels so good, and it's so tight."

"DJ don't stop please, don't stop."

"Tell daddy how good it feels, tell daddy."

"You feel so good."

"Is this my pussy?"

"Yessssss, DJ its yourssssss!"

"It's my what, Imani?"

"It's your pussy, DJ. It's yours. I promise it's yours. I'm cumin', DJ. I'm cummin'!"

"That's it, cum on daddy's dick. Just like that, cum for me baby girl."

DJ was really marking his territory with each stroke.

"Don't run from me. Take this dick. You wanted it now take it like a big girl. You running like you want me to stop. You want me to stop?"

"No, Darius please don't stop."

"Oh, so I'm Darius now?"

"Ahhhhhh, Darius I'm cummin'! DJ, don't stop please!"

"Can you cum one more time for me? Cum with me, baby girl."

"DJ I'm cumin', I'm cumin'!"

After a few more strokes, DJ and I came together, and it was the best feeling I had ever experienced. DJ slowly pulled out of me and walked to the bathroom to remove the condom. I grabbed my blanket and sat up in the bed. My mind was all over the place. I had just lost my virginity to a man I hardly knew, but it was the best feeling in the world. I had a million questions going through my head, and I really wanted to break down and cry, but I didn't want DJ to look at me differently.

DJ finally came out of the bathroom holding a wet towel. He removed the blanket from my body and began to gently wipe my pussy. He made small circles around the outside of my pussy and gently toyed with my throbbing clit. I flinched a little because I was sore as fuck, which made DJ laugh a little. DJ finished cleaning me up and climbed in the bed with me and pulled me close to him. For a few moments, we both just laid in each other's arms quietly.

"What's on your mind, Imani?"

"I'm not sure, but it's a lot."

"What do you mean? You can talk to me about anything."

"I guess I am just a little nervous and scared, I really like you DJ, and I don't want you to think of me any differently because I wanted to sleep with you. I don't want this to be the last time I am with you. I don't want to be hurt."

"Imani, I told you before we had sex that if you chose to have sex with me you were mine, and there is no turning back. I am pretty sure you have never been with a street nigga, but we are very territorial about ours, and I promise to protect you and never hurt or allow anyone else to hurt you. I don't give a fuck who it is, not to mention that pussy is A-1, and I am the first to bust wide open. You have nothing to worry about. Now let's lay down. I got you, Imani."

It was something about the way he said he got me, made believe him.

DARIUS

I woke up the next morning with Imani lying on my chest. She looked so beautiful sleeping. Last night was the first night I slept all night in a very long time. I even turned my phone completely off. Shit happened so fast last night. I didn't plan on fucking, but she wanted it, and I damn sure did too. However, I was willing to wait until she was ready. Knowing that I was the first one to feel that pussy had a nigga feeling himself a little bit.

I slightly tugged at Imani to wake her up. Even fresh out of her sleep she was flawless from the hairs out of place to the way that she tried to get her eyes to focus.

"Good morning," Imani softly spoke. "Would you like for me to fix you something eat or do you want something to drink?"

"Nah baby girl, I got a few moves to make today."

"Oh ok, I understand."

"Don't look like that. You will see me again today. You gotta trust me. Do you trust me, Imani?"

"Yes DJ, I trust you."

"What are your plans today, baby girl?"

"Nothing really besides going to my parent's house. My father and brother are going on a trip this weekend, so I will just go see them off then come back and study

"How bout I come back tonight, and you can make me dinner?"

"I would like that, DJ."

"Good now come on and take a shower with me and send your man off happy."

"But I'm sore, DJ."

"That just means I did you right."

***

About an hour later, we were both dressed, and I was headed towards the door. I kissed Imani passionately and headed out the door. I made her a promise that I was coming back, and I had every intention to do just that. I had some business to handle today, but I was definitely coming back tonight. I checked my phone and saw that I had missed calls from Zay, Marcus, and Kase. I also had text messages from Janae. I knew that she was upset and would probably cuss my ass out, but I didn't care. I was cutting her no good ass off anyway. I was pretty sure I found my queen. I just had to take over this business and make shit official. I hooked up my phone to the Bluetooth in my car and called Zay first.

"What's up, nigga?" I asked Zay once he answered

"Ain't shit where the fuck you been? I have been calling your pussy whipped ass all night. I figured your begging ass was somewhere begging for some pussy."

"First off all bitch I don't beg for pussy, and stop worrying about my dick. Now, what's up?"

"Well if your whining ass would have answered your phone you would know that Kase is looking for you. He is leaving today and needs the merchandise."

"Damn, I forgot he was leaving today. I'll be there in ten minutes I'm headed in the direction of Destiny now."

Few people knew I had ties to the Carolinas, and I wanted to keep it that way for a while. I had enough hate in my own city, so I always kept a low profile down south. Since Kase's pops was from the Queen city and he had family in North and South Carolina he was the go-to for the south. Eventually, I would have the entire east coast on lock, but that was a process that I wasn't quite ready for yet. I arrived at Destiny about twenty minutes later. Although I saw Zay standing outside, I still did the same routine that I did every time I came to the trap. I checked my surroundings and grabbed my gun.

"What's up, nigga? where everybody at?"

"Shit it's just Kase and me for now. Marcus left a few minutes ago. Me and Kase were discussing his trip to the south, and Marcus just up and left like a little bitch. Maybe his period on or some shit cause he acting real feminine today. Meanwhile, Kase's ole bitch ass is in there crying to Kaya, ole cry baby ass nigga."

"You hell, Zay."

"Shit, I know that. Now let's go get this shit so that we can send cry baby ass Kase on his way. I'm bout sick of y'all love sick motherfuckers. Y'all are fucking kings of the street and crying over pussy. What type of fuck boy shit is that?"

"Kase, what's up boy, I heard you in here crying and bitching. Kaya must have cut your ass off."

"Man fuck you, DJ. Get me the shit so I can go. Pops and I are driving down tonight."

"Ight bet, let's go in the back."

"Zay, did that nigga Marcus say where he was going? He just up and left and didn't say shit?

"Like I told you we were talking about the Carolina trip and he just grabbed his phone and walked off. I don't know what the nigga problem is."

"Yeah, that nigga's been acting real funny for a minute, DJ. You and Zay had better watch that nigga."

"I don't know what the fuck is going on with that nigga. Let's get you this shit packed up so you and your pops can head out.

Just like all the other trips that Kase took down south, we packed enough of the product to last. We loaded the product and money in Kase's Camaro, and we made sure we had the burner phones for his trip. A lot of shit didn't seem right. Kase was usually hyped about his Carolina runs, but this time, he seemed like he wasn't feeling it. That shit that Marcus told me about that nigga was replaying in my head. Then, on the other hand, that nigga Marcus had been acting funny as well. All I know is they better not fuck with my money.

"Let me holler at you right quick, DJ."

"Alright what's up?"

"Some shit ain't adding up. Some money and product count are missing, and we need to get to the bottom of this. Only a few have access to Destiny, so it's someone close. Now you know the one thing I don't fuck with is a liar and thief. That shit will get you killed fucking with my money."

"Are you sure, Zay?"

"What you mean am I sure? I wouldn't bring the shit up if I weren't sure, DJ. Shit ain't right, and I think shit ain't been right for a minute."

"Well we need to get to the bottom of some shit then, and we need to start with them lil niggas on the corners."

"Nah, I don't think it's them lil soldiers. This shit is inside."

Alright, well let's call a meeting next week and try to get some type of information."

"That's what's up. If we gone take over, then we need to eliminate all fuck boys and snakes. We got enough hate on the street to have them in our own crew."

"I feel you on that shit Zay. These niggas know I don't play about my fucking money and if they stealing my shit, then it's nighty night for that motherfucker."

"Big facts, let's go try and get an estimate of what's missing."

***

Hours after counting money and product, it was an estimate of about twenty thousand dollars missing between the product and the money. That shit had me furious. Who the fuck would have the fucking balls to come up in my shit and steal from me? On my momma when I find out who the fuck it was, they gone die. I blamed myself for not staying on top of shit like I should have, but with the new connect and taking over from pops that have been my main focus. Shit was about to get real.

"What you thinking, DJ?"

"The fuck am I supposed to think, Zay? Twenty thousand of product and money just vanished. I should just start laying niggas out to prove my fucking point about my money."

"I have had my eye on Marcus for a while. That nigga is always here but don't be doing shit, and the way his bitch ass walked out today was straight suspect.

"Well, if that nigga got anything to do with my shit coming up missing, he's dead, and I put that on my momma."

"Fuck yeah, I text that nigga and his ass didn't text me back, but when he does I got some fucking questions for his ass."

This shit had me fucking furious right now. I made sure that my entire team was eating just as good as me, so for a motherfucker to come up and take my shit had me ready to lay niggas out. Not only did I have to worry about nigga stealing my shit, but now to take my shit and start selling it in my fucking city. I was trying to prevent bloodshed, but niggas were forcing me to bring out that savage ass side of me.

XAVIER

Shit down at the trap was fucked up. Twenty fucking thousand in money and fucking drugs just gone, how the fuck did that shit happen? I had to figure that shit. I had a bad feeling about Marcus. That nigga's been acting real suspect for a while. I just kept my thoughts to myself until I was sure. DJ had loyalty for that nigga since they grew up together, so I didn't want to come to him about what I suspected until I was for sure, but now I was convinced that nigga was a snake. DJ was big on loyalty and to see my best friend get burned by a nigga that he was loyal to him had me ready to blow that motherfucker's brains all over DC.

I left DJ at the trap since I promised my baby I would come by and get her. I hated to disappoint my seed, so I made sure when I said I was coming, I came through. Although Kamya was only two-years-old, I still hated to break promises to her. Today I was going to take my baby shopping. She had a birthday coming up, so it was time to drop a few stacks. I could easily just give Jada the money, but I didn't trust my baby mama not to spend some of the money on her and her hoe ass sister, which would give me even more reason to kill her ass.

I sent Jada a text to let her know to get Kamya dressed, and that I was on the way, I just hoped she did it because I wasn't trying to stay around her people for longer than I had to. I made it to Jada's spot about thirty minutes after I sent the text, and with my luck, Jada had Mya dressed and ready to go. I had to admit she had my baby looking beautiful. Mya was dressed in a blue denim jumper with a red shirt underneath along with her red Chuck Taylor's. Her hair was braided really cute with red ribbons and bows. I will always admit the one thing we did great together was make a beautiful child.

"How long are you keeping her, Zay?"

"Don't worry about that. I will bring her back in a day or two."

"I think I should know how long my child will be gone. Is that too much to ask, Zay?"

"Look, Jada. Don't start that shit. I told you I would keep her for a day or two."

"Zay, it's whatever. I try to have a civilized conversation with you and you blow me off."

"We don't have shit to talk about, Jada."

I ended the conversation with Jada right before it started. There was nothing there between us other than Mya, so there was no need to have no type of conversation. I grabbed Mya and her bags, got in my car, and drove off.

I was prepared for a daddy-daughter day with my princess. Anything she wanted daddy was gone get her. Mya and I ended up at one of the malls in uptown DC. This mall had it all even a Chuck E Cheese, which was Mya's favorite place in the entire world. Every time we passed this place, she wanted to stop, and of course, I gave in.

***

Three hours later, Mya was in her stroller knocked out like she had just worked a twelve-hour day. The shopping wasn't so bad, but the Chuck E Cheese wore her and me out. I knew it was time to go, but a nigga was hungry.

"Your daughter is beautiful," I heard someone say.

I turned around and saw Brianna standing behind me looking beautiful as ever. Brianna was the last person I expected to see today, but damn, she was looking fine as hell in that pink outfit. We exchanged number at the club that night, but I didn't expect to run into her so soon. I wasn't looking for no type of relationship or no shit like that, but I wouldn't mind fucking with Bri. Shorty was bad as fuck, and her body was crazy.

"Damn, what's up, Brianna? I didn't know you lived around here?"

"I don't. I live closer to Georgetown University where I go to school. I was only on this side of town because I needed something for school and only a certain store sold it, and it was quicker to come here than drive further south.

"That's what's up. Shit, you wanna sit and have lunch with us."

"Nah, I gotta get back, but it was good seeing you again."

"Yeah, same here, Bri. See you later."

"See you later, Zay."

Damn, watching Bri walk away had me wanting to call her back and invite her over for the night, but I didn't. Tonight was about my baby. I grabbed my food and Mya, and I headed home for the night.

***

Later that night Kamya was out for the count. When we made it home, I let her run her little self tired. I really enjoyed seeing my seed just laugh and have fun. I swear she was hyped for about five hours until she finally started to wind down. That was my cue to get her washed and ready for bed. To my surprise, she didn't put up a fight to go to sleep. I laid on my couch with my baby laying on my chest with a million and one thoughts going through my head. This shit with DJ and the work had me all the fucked up, but I had to play that shit smart. Now was not the time to be reckless. I also thought about Brianna. Maybe it was time for me to try to find someone else. I would never tell DJ that he was right, but he was. These late nights got lonely, and I honestly wanted to come home for a home cooked meal and a beautiful woman.

I laid Mya down in her bed and decided to hit up Brianna, not on some I'm trying to fuck type shit but just to chill and get to know her a little bit. Fuck it. I grabbed my phone and sent her a text asking her what she up to. It was either hit or miss from here. I was gone try this dating shit one last time, and if the shit failed this time, then fuck I'll just fuck until my dick falls off.

Imani

"Hey, Brianna, what's up?"

"Don't hey Bri what's up me. Here it is Monday, you had your date with DJ two days ago, and you couldn't even call me and tell me how it went or nothing. What type of best friend are you? Now spill the tea, how did it go?"

"Bri there is nothing to tell. We had a great time, and he left the next morning."

"Bitch shut up, he stayed the night? So you fucked him? Bitch you fucked him, was it good?

"Bri he was amazing, I didn't think my body would feel like that. The way he took his time with me was so sexy Bri, and don't get me not start on his head game."

"Bitch, so you got fucked for real. It's bout time you let your hair down and bust that pussy open."

"Oh my god, Bri. Why you gotta be so nasty?"

"You already know why that is cause I'm nasty. I'm just glad that you finally let somebody play in that pussy. Now you can loosen up a little and enjoy life. "

"I know how to enjoy life Brianna, but other than you insulting my life, how have you been? How was your weekend of nonstop studying?

"Boring as hell, but I had to get it done. I did wake up this morning with a text from Zay though."

"Wait Bri, how does he have your number?"

"The night in the club when you and DJ were in the car for hours, we kind of kicked and exchanged numbers, but I don't think I can get to serious with him. He's got a kid, Imani."

"How do you know he got a kid?"

"Because I came across his Instagram and saw a picture he posted with her, and I ran into him in the mall, and he was with her. You know I can't fuck with no man with a baby and a baby mama."

"Bri, give him a chance. He might surprise you."

"Imani, no I'm not dealing with that, that's why I didn't text him back."

"Well, Bri answer this. How are you going to give me advice about taking chances and you not follow your own advice?"

"Because my situation is different now drop it."

"Alright fine Bri, with your stubborn ass. I won't say nothing else. I'll simply say that I will talk to you later. I am headed to my parents' house. See you later."

I hung up with Brianna and headed to my parents. I really needed to have a talk with all of my siblings before getting our parents involved. Kassem and my dad had returned from their trip to Charlotte, so I would have to reach out to Kase about a sit down with our siblings. This weekend had been nothing short of amazing. DJ kept his promise and came back that night. I cooked for him as I promised and again he made my body feel so damn good. I still had a hard time processing the fact that I had lost my virginity and now had a boyfriend all in the same weekend.

Arriving at my parent's house a few minutes later, I didn't see Kaseem's car in the driveway.

"Damn it. That boy just don't do right."

I called Kase's phone, and of course, I was sent to voicemail.

"Kase, we need to sit down with the twins to see what they got going on before getting mommy and daddy involved. Could you please call me back." I just hoped he called me back soon. I was really concerned about my siblings

"Hey mommy," I greeted my mother like I always did. "Where is everyone?"

"I am not sure, Imani. Major's been gone most of the day, and Marie is over that lil girl's house she always at, Katina or something. I haven't seen Kase since him and your daddy got back from their trip, but what is going on with you, Imani? You look different, and you're glowing a little, baby. Did you meet someone and been hiding it from me?"

"Mommy, I am not glowing. I look the same. If anything the stress of school has me drained."

"No you met someone, I'm your mother I know everything about each and every one of you."

"Yes mommy, I did meet someone, but it's nothing major right now we're just getting to know each other and taking things slow."

"Ok, Imani take things slow alright. The boy whoever he is done, tap that cause you walking funny. Is he someone at school?"

"Oh my god mommy, and no he is not someone at school."

"Don't act like that, baby. I was young once, and I remember when I met your father, and he took my virginity, I had that same glow and that same walk. It's nothing to be shocked about, baby. Mama knows everything. Trust me."

I really couldn't keep anything from my mother, so it was hard for me not to tell her what I knew about the twins. I just really wanted to get all the facts first. Honestly, this was stressing me out. Kase was the oldest, and he wasn't any help. Yeah, I know he was dealing with his personal issues and graduation coming up soon, but I really needed him with me on this. I contemplated dropping hints on my mother, but I just couldn't do. I had to be one hundred percent certain, and with my mom being a lawyer and Major supposedly selling drugs, things could get real ugly.

I left my parents' house more stressed than when I got there, I still hadn't heard from Kase or DJ all day, and I didn't want to take all my problems to Brianna. The only place that I knew I could go and just clear my mind was the library. I headed to school to study for midterms that I had coming up. At least I could get my mind off family drama for a while and focus on school.

DARIUS

So much shit had been happening for the past few days, and the fact that there was a snake in my camp had me fucked up. Right now, every fucking body was suspect. I honestly didn't give a fuck who it was. Nggas were gone get this work. I was calling a meeting to let niggas know that I knew what was up and that shit wasn't going to fly, and when I find out who the motherfucker is that has the fucking balls to steal from me, then it was fucking over for him. The only nigga I felt I could trust was Zay everybody else was fucking suspect. Not only did I have to find out who the fuck the snake ass nigga was, but I also had to explain that shit to my pops and Emmanuel. This shit couldn't get any fucking worse.

I called Zay, Kase, and Marcus and had them to round up the soldiers and workers and meet at the spot. I hadn't heard from my lil shorty all day, and I had to get my mind right before I pulled up, but I sent her a text to let her know once I finished taking care of business I would stop by. Now it was time to handle business, I grabbed my guns and headed to the meeting spot.

Pulling up to the spot, I noticed everybody but Marcus was there. That was strike number one for that man. Everybody in my camp knew that if I called a meeting, stop what the fuck you doing and let's get shit handled.

"Zay, where that nigga Marcus at?"

"Fuck if I know, I called and text that nigga bout five times."

"That nigga is fucking up bad, and why the fuck Kase over there looking like his whole world about to end?"

"DJ, I don't fucking know what the fuck his problem is. I had to cut my time short with Kamya for this meeting, so these motherfuckers better not be on that bullshit cause my trigger finger is itching right now

"Yo, calm the fuck down, Zay. We can't be reckless."

"Man fuck that, let's just do this shit."

"So we called this meeting because it seems like someone has a problem with keeping their fucking hands off my shit. I make sure that every fucking one in this house eats and eats good, so why is it that someone feels the need to steal from me? I don't know who it was but trust me I will find out, and when I do, you better hope I'm not in a fucked up mood and decide to let you live.

When I first put everyone on the first thing I said was never fucking steal or fucking lie to me, and here we are a fucking thief in my crew. Just know when I find out who the fuck it is it's over for you. Now you all can go. I just wanted to make whoever it is that has the balls to pull this off aware of it, so whatever the fuck you think you're doing, that shit ain't go fly. I need everyone is this meeting to keep their ear to the streets, and whatever it is let me or Zay know what's up. Keep us up with everything you hear. We gone switch it up little bit, so be prepared for some changes. Y'all can go, I'm done."

I ended the meeting because I didn't plan on dragging shit out. I wanted to get to the fucking point and keep that shit moving. I needed to go and holla at my pops about what the fuck was going on and then head on over to my shorty's house. I really needed her to be my peace right now. I was stressed like a motherfucker.

"Let me holla at you right quick, DJ."

"Alright what's up, Kase?

"So check it, I don't know how much you know, but you need to keep your eye on Marcus, bruh. I am trying to tell you that nigga is a snake, and I know he be in here late at night because I saw his car her late one night coming from Kaya's house, and he wasn't alone. He had some other nigga with him. I didn't get a good look at the dude, but he wasn't anyone from our crew."

"Why didn't you say shit earlier or put Zay or me on so that we could check that nigga?"

"Cause I wanted to be sure first before sayin' shit, but I told y'all that nigga been moving funny for a minute."

"Yeah you did, and I appreciate that, but now it's about catching that nigga. They gone lay low for a minute now that they know we on that ass, but they gone slip again, and when they do, it's a fucking wrap."

"I also wanted to let you know that I'm falling back. I'm about to invest in this sports bar with my pops. I'm not saying that I'm done with this street shit because I know I will never been completely done with it, but I need to fall back and get this shit legit. Making this money legally was something me you and Zay always talked about, but lately, y'all not trying to make this move, so I'm taking it upon myself to do it."

"So what you saying, Kase, you stepping down, at a time like this? You bitching up and stepping down? What the fuck is going on with this team?"

"Ain't no body bitching up DJ, so kill that shit.

"That's what the fuck it sounds like to me, a fucking bitch ass move."

"DJ, what the fuck is going on?" Zay yelled.

"I don't fucking know what's going. It's bad enough mutherfuckers got big fucking balls to steal from me, and now this nigga hollering bout he stepping down to start up a fucking sports bar at a fucking time like this. When I need the team to be strong, he's bitching up!"

"Look, DJ. It ain't gone be too much more of you insulting me."

"And what the fuck you gone do about, Kasseem."

"Look, I know you got a lot going on, and you're not thinking straight, so I'm gone let that shit you talking go, but watch how you fucking come at me."

"Whoa, both of you calm the fuck down. We supposed to be a unit that these lil cats look up to and here the two of you out here arguing like some bitches. Kase, you could have done that shit at a better time, and DJ you need to calm the fuck down!"

"Calm the fuck down Zay, coming from somebody who shoots first and think later. Get the fuck outta here with that shit."

I got in my car and drove the fuck off. The more I stood there, the more I wanted to off that nigga. At a fucking time like this, he wanted to make shit legit. The fuck kind of shit is that? I was looking at that nigga sideways now. I wasn't in the fucking mood to deal with my pops right now. I would handle that shit tomorrow. I was headed over to Imani's place. I just hoped shit didn't get worse from here on out.

I sent Imani a text and told her I was on my way. I hoped she wasn't feeling some type away from me not calling her all day. Right now, I just wanted to be in her presence, not on no just fucking type shit either. I just enjoyed her company. In just that short time Imani was everything I was looking for— sexy as fuck, smart, independent, and she was definitely the shit. I wanted shorty in the worst way, but I wasn't trying to look and sound all desperate and shit. Before heading into Imani's spot, I had to roll up. I needed my daily dose to clear my head. I wasn't trying to take that negative energy with me in Imani's crib. After taking one to the head, I headed up to Imani's apartment. Whatever she was cooking smelled so good that made me realize that I hadn't eaten anything all day. Imani opened the door looking just as beautiful as ever. I could definitely get used to this, coming home to a beautiful woman and a home cook meal.

Jamie Marie

Kaseem

I knew DJ would react the way he did, that's no surprise. Because we are boys, I didn't go in his mouth for the way he was talking to me. Maybe this was not the best time to step the fuck down, but I figured I needed to do it now. Pops and I already invested money, so there was no turning back. I was graduating in three weeks, so I needed to get my shit together and now was the time. I would let DJ cool down then maybe we could sit down and have a conversation, but right now, I was headed to Imani's spot. She'd called me a few times today, but I was too caught up with DJ's meeting and then our conversation I just didn't have time to call her back. I already knew what she wanted to talk about.

We still haven't had another conversation with the twins or our parents. I needed to see who my little brother was supposedly running drugs for and put an end to that shit quickly. I didn't want Major caught up in that life at all. I would just have to keep my ears to the street. I pulled up to Imani's spot and didn't text her to let her know I was coming since I knew she would be home studying. That was my sister's life; school and studying were all she did. Walking up to my sister's apartment, whatever she was cooking smelled good. It looks like I came just in time.

"Kase, what's up, what's going on?"

"Nothing much, you called me earlier but I wasn't in the mood to talk, you busy?"

"No I'm not busy, but I have company, but you can come in. Have you eaten anything today?"

"No, I haven't eaten today."

"Come on in. I can fix you a plate."

"Aight, bet."

"Have you talked to the twins, Kase?"

"DJ, what the hell are you doing here? Imani, what is going on?"

"Kase, how do you know DJ?"

"Imani, it doesn't matter how I know him. Why is he here?"

"Hold up Imani, how do you know Kase?"

"DJ, Kase is my brother. Remember I told you I had three siblings."

"Your brother? Oh shit, seriously?"

"Yeah nigga, I am her big brother, so again how the fuck do you to know each other?"

"Well Kase, this is my woman."

"Your woman? Get the fuck out of here. Imani, what the fuck are you doing, do you even know him and know what he does Imani, or were you just ready to start fucking that you let anyone hit? What is it, Imani?"

"Kasseem, hold up. You are out of line. You are my brother, not my daddy, so watch how you talk to me."

"Just to make shit clear, Kase. Imani knows what I do. I let that be known before we started fucking, but I take it that she doesn't know that you work for me?"

"What! You work for him, Kase. What about school, what the hell is going on?"

"Yeah, Kase, tell her you work for me and how you have worked for me for three years."

"Fuck you, DJ. Imani, you're my sister, and I wouldn't tell you wrong, but you need to watch this nigga, I don't know what he told you, but he ain't nobody you wanna fuck with."

"If that's how you feel Kase then how do you know him and apparently working for him? Kase, I'm fine. I can handle myself, but how can you have a conversation with Major if you're doing the same thing? You have been lying to me all this time, so don't come at me about who I allow in my house or who I choose to be with."

"Do what you want to do Imani, but don't come to me crying, when this nigga dog you out."

"You mean the way you're doing Kaya or the way you do women period? You're the last one to give out advice for relationships, Kase."

"Imani, do what you do, I'm out."

"Darius, please explain this to me. What is going on?"

"Baby girl, let me put it to you like this. Your brother is not the perfect big brother you think he is. Kase has been on my team for years helping me to run these streets, and today we got into an argument, so I guess he still salty about the situation. The only reason I didn't go in his mouth is because of you, but whatever we had is dead, and if that's a problem for you let me know now, and I can step. As I told you I'm a street nigga, and any other nigga would be leaking on your floor right now, but Kase and I have history long history."

"What type of argument, DJ?" I need you to be straight up with me please."

"Nah baby girl, it's not my place. You need to speak to Kase about that."

"I need to call my brother."

***

What the fuck was really going on? When did Imani start fucking with DJ? What the fuck was she thinking fucking with a nigga like him? DJ and I got history, so I know this nigga's body count, so if he thinks he's adding my sister, he's got another fucking problem. The shit was fucked from all angles. I wonder who all knew DJ and Imani were fucking. I needed to hit up Zay and see how much he knew. Knowing him, his loyalty was to DJ. Fuck it. Let me hit this nigga line

Xavier

"**G**od damn, Bri, suck that shit fuck! I'm about to nut. I swear to God if you swallow that shit, you mine, on God. Fucccckkkkkk!!!!! Bri. Goddamn girl, not only is your pussy fire, but your head game is the shit. Where have you been all my life?"

"Boy, stop playing."

"I am dead ass. What you doing later? I need you to come back tonight."

"I don't have any plans later."

"Cool, I'm gone leave some money and a spare key on the dresser. Get us some food tonight, If I'm not here when you get back, just chill, or if you don't have any plans, you can chill here until I get back and just have Uber Eats bring something."

"Ummm ok, Zay."

"If you leave, just come back."

I ended up fucking with Bri after that shit went down at the meeting. Shit was getting stressful as fuck, and I needed some pussy and some head. I took a chance by calling up Bri. I was feeling shorty. I text her to meet up for some lunch, and shit, one thing led to another, and we were at my spot fucking. They say good pussy will have a nigga making promises and shit. Damn, I just invited her to stay at my spot while I handled some business and left her some money.

She was the fucking truth I should have known she was a bad bitch in bed from the way she danced at the club a few nights ago, but that was nothing compared to the way she put that pussy on my ass. I told her she could stay until I got back. I wanted to come back to the crib and play house.

As I finished getting dressed I thought about how I needed to head over to my mom's spot and pick up Mya. When DJ called his meeting that cut my time with Mya, so I took her to my mom's spot to keep from hearing Jada bitching. I wasn't ready to take her back home to Jada, so I decided just to get Mya and bring her back to my crib. I never let any female I was fucking be around my daughter, but I was taking a chance with Bri being there. If she didn't want to stay, it was cool, Mya and me could chill all by ourselves.

I didn't want to just pop back up with Mya and not say shit. I wanted to let Bri know first in case she wanted to go ahead and leave. I walked out the guest bathroom, and Bri was lying on my bed in one of my t-shirts looking so fucking sexy.

"I hope you don't mind I grabbed one of your tank shirts to throw on."

"Nah, Bri you're good, so you decided to stay, huh. Don't tell me the dick got you hooked already?"

"No Zay, you asked me to stay, and I don't have any plans today, so why not stay."

"Cool, I was headed out to get my daughter from my mom's house and bring her back. I understand if you don't want to stay if she is here if, so we can hook up some other time."

"I don't mind, Zay. I just don't want to cause no trouble between you and your baby mama. Trust me. I ain't trying to go to jail for beating a bitch over a man who ain't even mine."

"You're not mine yet officially, but you don't got to worry about my baby mama. We're not even rocking like that. I just tolerate her ass for the sake of our daughter. I honestly can't stand that bitch."

I meant every word I said. I don't know why but I just felt like I needed to be straight up with Bri. Shit, the fuck was that all about. I left Brianna at the house sleep, just as I said I left her some money to get us some food. I could take Kamya home to Jada, but I wasn't ready for my baby to leave just yet. I needed to spend more time with Maya. I didn't want her to grow up and me not be around. Just because I couldn't stand her mama, it didn't mean my baby had to suffer.

Getting into my car, I thought about some of the things that DJ was telling me about settling down, and I had to admit he was right, but of course, I would never tell his conceited ass that. I wanted that family with the big house on the hill and the white Pickett fence one day. I heard my phone ringing, and I just knew it was my mama or my sisters calling me, but it was Kase. I could only imagine what the fuck he wanted. That shit that went down with him and DJ was wild as fuck.

"Kase, what's up man?"

"Ain't shit, Zay I got a question for you. How long has DJ been fucking my baby sister?"

"Kase, what the fuck is you talking about, who is your sister?"

"Imani. I just left my sister's house and who the fuck is laid up with her but DJ."

"Oh shit, Imani is your sister? Say word, yo that's fucking wild, I swear we had no idea."

"Shit, how the fuck did they meet?"

"Look, Kase. That ain't my place to tell they business. If they want to talk to you about it, then they will."

"You know what Zay fuck it. I forgot your loyalty would be with DJ no matter what."

This shit was getting crazier by the minute. What were the odds that Imani would be Kase's little sister of all people? I needed to call DJ and see what the fuck was up. I called DJ's number, and of course, it went straight to voicemail.

"DJ, what the fuck is going on, is Imani really Kase's sister? Y'all need to squash that shit for real, hit my line back, man."

I was at a lost right now. Shit was getting out of hand. All I knew was that we had work to do. At the end of the day we all had to eat, and I wasn't about to let those two stop me and mine from eating. It's bad enough that we had a snake on our team. We didn't need the beefing between two of the main niggas in the crew. Shit had to be worked out. We had a possible war on our hands once we found out who the fuck was stealing from us. All I know was that shit needed to get back on track and fast.

I headed to my mom's spot to get Kamya. I was going to end the rest of my day with my baby and Bri. I didn't know what to expect, but I would enjoy my day with the ladies and prepare myself for what's to come tomorrow

IMANI

I still had so many unanswered questions going through my head. After the conversation with Kase and DJ, I was still so confused. If Kase was working for DJ, then how did he have time for school? Was Kase still in school? I knew what DJ did for a living. He was one hundred percent honest with me from the start, and he gave me the option to walk away if I wanted to, but I chose not to. Never in a million year would I think that my own brother was doing the same thing. It just didn't make any sense to me. I needed to have a conversation with both my brother and DJ. I was kind of new to this relationship thing, so I didn't know where to start. They were friends before me, and I wasn't trying to be in the middle of that.

Right now, I needed to talk to Brianna. I just needed to vent and make this make sense. I called Bri's phone, and surprisingly, she was home and awake. I was glad cause I was pulling up to her campus dorm as I called.

"Imani, what are you doing here so early?

"I need to talk to you. Are you busy, please say you're not busy?"

"No, I'm not busy. I'm just getting home but not busy. What's going on? Don't tell me it the twins again."

"No Bri, it's not the twins. It's Kase."

"Ok, what's wrong with Kase? Imani, you're scaring me."

"Well apparently DJ and Kase are friends or business partners, and Kase has been working for DJ for about three years. They got into some sort of argument, and Kase found out about me and DJ, and now they both are going at."

"Imani stop, back the hell up. They know each other and Kase works for DJ, doing what?

"Ok, don't say anything but DJ sells drugs, and apparently, Kase has been for the last three years."

"Wait a damn minute, Imani. You knew that DJ is a street nigga and you still fucked with him? Girl, he must have some good dick."

"Bri, it's not about the sex or nothing like that."

"Imani, calm down, why is this making you so upset? Obviously they had a fallen out before Kase knew about y'all, so what is the problem?"

"One of my main problems is that Kase has been lying to me for so long, I thought we were better than that, then on top of that, how is he supposed to help me have a conversation with Major if he's doing the same damn thing?"

"Yeah, Mani I see your point. That's some hypocritical type shit there, but if Kase and DJ are friends, then that means Kase and Zay are cool also, damn."

"I guess Bri, but what does Zay have to do with this?"

"Remember I told you that I was just getting home, well I was with Zay and his daughter."

"This is getting crazier by the minute. How did you and Zay hook up, and how long have y'all been seeing each other?"

"Look, that's not important. I tell you what you call DJ and ask him to dinner tonight, I will call Zay, and the four of us can go out tonight and just chill. This has been some long crazy last few days.

"Yeah I guess that's ok, I will let you know what he says."

"No Imani, make him say yes, ok."

"Ok Bri fine, I will tell him. You chose a place, and we will be there."

Maybe this little dinner date will shine some light on the situations. I don't want to come in between a friendship with Kase and DJ, so I will just ask DJ to tell me what's going on. I know Kase's stubborn ass won't willingly tell me. Maybe just maybe they can work things out.

I left Brianna's place so that I could run to the school for a while. I needed to start on a paper for my medical terminology class, but I needed to get some more information from my professor. I called DJ on the way to campus, but all I got was he voicemail. I left him a message asking him to call me back so that we can discuss tonight's dinner date. I was praying he would call me back. We didn't really speak much last night or this morning when everything went down with him and Kase. I just wanted everything to go back to normal, but maybe that was wishful thinking on my part.

As soon as I made it to campus, I saw the one person I didn't want to see, Aaron. I didn't feel like dealing with Aaron and his begging me to go out with him, so I will just have to let him down.

"What's up beautiful?"

"Hey Aaron, what's up?"

"Nothing I just came here to get some information for a paper, that's it."

"So if I recall right, you said that we could have dinner after midterms, and midterms are next week, so when can I expect that dinner date, Ms. Imani?"

"Look, Aaron. I don't know about dinner, I'm kind of seeing someone right now. It's new, but I want to take things slow with him."

"Oh, so when did this take place, if you don't mind me asking?"

"As I told you, Aaron. It's new, and we are just getting to know each other."

"Well, how long have you known this mystery guy, Imani cause if I'm not mistaken it was just a few weeks ago we made these plans your backing out of now."

"Look, Aaron. It just happened, and I apologize, but I hope we can remain friends."

"Friends, yeah whatever. Enjoy your little boyfriend, Imani."

The way Aaron stormed off I had a feeling he was done with me for good, which I guess was best in the end. He always tried to force me to go out with him. I know we had our little thing in the past, but I never developed any type of feelings for him. I was just ready to get this day over with and talk to DJ. He still hadn't texted or called me back yet. I just hoped that things with us were good.

I made it to the room with my professor and got the material that I needed to start my paper. I decided to stay on campus for a while to get some research done. This was a huge paper that was worth eighty percent of my midterm grade, so I had to find a way to focus and get it done."

DARIUS

S hit was all fucked up. I hadn't talked to baby girl since last night. After that shit went down between Kase and me, we just went to bed not saying much. I know she had a lot to process everything with Kasem and me, especially Kase. I was straight up with her from the start, but to find out that her big brother was lying for so long was flaw. I could see the pain in her face, and I wanted to comfort her and make her talk to me, but I wasn't trying to force her. However, baby girl needed to understand that being with me communication is the key, but I would give her space for now, but later we would have a conversation.

Right now, I was riding through the city with a million things going through my mind. I had just had a talk with Zay about last night. Apparently Kase had called him and told him about Imani and me. Kase said some really fucked up shit last night and like I told him, if we didn't have the history that we had, he would be leaking everywhere. The one thing I didn't tolerate was disrespect. I was so lost in my thoughts that I hadn't checked my phone in about an hour. I noticed that Imani called me and left a voicemail. I was glad she did, I miss lil mama. On the voicemail, she said something about dinner tonight with Zay and Brianna. Zay did mention that he and Brianna were messing around. I called my baby back and told her that would be fine, and I was looking forward to it.

I was now headed to my pops spot to have a conversation with him and Emmanuel about what has transpired in the last few days with the missing money and drugs. This was a conversation I was dreading, but if I was going to run this city and the entire east coast, I needed to get it done and reassure Emmanuel that his product was good with me, and I was in it to make him and myself a lot of fucking money.

***

Imani was looking so sexy in that dress, and if we didn't have dinner reservations, I would rip that dress off of her and lay her on the counter, but I knew she wasn't having it. Right now we were headed to dinner with Zay and Brianna, and Imani was really looking forward to this dinner. She'd had a pretty rough last few days. I just wanted to make my baby happy.

"Are you ready, DJ?"

"Sure thing beautiful, let's go enjoy our night."

"Thank you, DJ, for doing this with me tonight. It really means a lot. I really just want to clear my head. I know you have a lot going on with my brother, and I don't want to be a distraction to you, DJ."

"Imani, why would you think you are a distraction? If I felt you were a distraction, we wouldn't be here right now. I have had my share of females around me Imani, but I haven't had the connection with any of them like I have for you. We have a connection, and I really want to build on that, but communication is the key. I know the shit that went down with Kase shocked you, but don't shut down on me. Let's keep the lines open, baby girl."

"I understand."

"Good now give me a kiss so that we can get this night over with and come back to my place for the night."

The ride to the restaurant was fairly quiet. I let the sounds of 112 flow through the car speakers as my lady and me rode through the city to our destination. I really just wanted to enjoy the night with my lady, take her home, and sex her all night. Had it been up to me we would have stayed home, but again, baby girl wanted to have this night, and I wanted to make her happy.

Imani had chosen a nice steak restaurant, which surprised me. She remembered that I loved steak even though she wasn't a big steak fan herself. When we arrived Zay and Brianna were already there waiting for us. I gotta admit my nigga was looking kind of fly with a Brianna with him. Maybe he was trying to take my advice about getting a woman, but who knows with him.

I stepped out of my car making sure I had my gun of course and ran over to open the door for Imani. The way the full moon shined on her face was breathtaking. She wore her hair in a natural curly style that made her look so amazing. I definitely had the baddest female in the restaurant and probably all of DC. The vibe for the night was definitely calm and mellow. The girls conversed while Zay and I talked business and the food was good as fuck. About an hour into our dinner, I looked over at Imani and saw that her entire mood had changed. She now had this worried look on her face, and she had turned a pale color.

"Imani, what wrong?"

"Kase is here. We can go, DJ."

"Nah Imani, I'm good. As long as nothing fucked up comes out of his mouth, we good."

I meant what I said as along as he kept his distance, shit would be good. The last thing I needed was for this nigga to act a fool in this restaurant and I have to lay him out in front of his sister, but if he pushed me, then so fucking be it.

"Imani, I thought I told you to watch out for this nigga."

"Kaseem, I am fine, and I don't appreciate you telling me what to do. Obviously, he is not that bad of a person you've been working for him for three years, so what's the problem? If y'all got issues, leave me out of it."

"Nah baby girl, ain't no issues. Kase, you a bitch and you lucky we are in this restaurant, and I don't lay your ass out."

"Fuck you, DJ. What the fuck you wanna do?"

"Whoa both of Y'all niggas chill the fuck out. It's too much heat right now, so we gone bounce, but Kase you fucking up, man. We been nothing but family to you, especially DJ, so I suggest you calm the fuck down and remember who the fuck been there for you, man. You can't let a little disagreement cause y'all to act like y'all ain't be boys for years. Just like I told DJ, y'all need to talk this shit through."

"Or what Zay, you been riding this nigga dick for years."

"You know what Kase, Marcus was right about you. You a fucking clown man and not worth my freedom, but I will see you again my nigga, bet on that."

"Fuck you DJ, and as for Marcus, if you were handling business and not fucking my sister you would know that nigga Marcus is the one stealing your shit, so now whose the clown?"

"The fuck you just say, Kase?"

"You heard what the fuck I said, DJ. That nigga's been the one stealing your shit."

By the time Imani could grab my arm, I was out the door and headed towards my car. I could hear Zay and Imani coming behind me, but right now I needed to find Marcus. By the time I got to my car, Imani had reached me with tears in her eyes, I looked at her, but now I needed to handle business.

"Darius, can we just go, please?"

"Nah baby girl, you take my car, and you and Brianna go back to your place. I will call you later."

I kissed Imani and got into Zay's car. He knew what time it was. I was headed to find Marcus. That nigga had to pay. I didn't see Kase come out of the restaurant, but that nigga's car was right behind us, I wonder what the fuck he was up too.

"Yo, why the fuck is that nigga following us, Zay?"

"The fuck if I know, but I don't have time to deal with his shit. That nigga Marcus got to fucking pay. I had a feeling about that nigga."

"Shit, Zay who the fuck is that coming up beside Kase?"

"Who the fuck is that? That car looks familiar…"

POW! POW! POW!

IMANI

I just stood there in shock as DJ and Zay drove off, and I didn't know what to think. Everything happened so fast. I don't know what the hell happened to Kase. I have never seen him act like that. The dark look in DJ's eyes scared me. *What had I gotten myself into?*

"Imani, come on. Let's get out of here and go back to your place until DJ or Zay calls us."

"Bri what the fuck just happened, like honestly what have I gotten myself into?"

"You're fucking with a street nigga, Mani. Let's just get out of here."

I handed Brianna the keys. I couldn't drive. My nerves were gone, I checked my phone to see if I had a message from DJ or Kase, but nothing. We pulled out of the parking lot and drove towards my apartment in silence. Not five minutes down the road, we hear gunshots followed by a loud boom.

POW! POW! POW! POW!

"Oh my god, Bri! What was that?"

"That sounded like gunshots."

"Oh my god, DJ!"

Brianna made quick U-turn and headed towards the direction of the gunshots.

Pulling up to the where we heard the gunshots, I couldn't believe my eyes. I didn't see Zay's car at first, but what I saw sent me into total shock.

"OH MY GOD, KASE! KASEEEEE!!!!"

TO BE CONTINUED

CPSIA information can be obtained
at www.ICGtesting.com
Printed in the USA
LVHW091759100219
607039LV00001B/21/P